What Othe

"This brilliant book of wisdom and life lessons, is carefully hidden in the disguise of a beautiful story, half poetry and half magic. It takes the reader on a journey through time, culture, spirit and space—rich with beauty, mystery and understanding."

—**Jonathan Ellerby, PhD**, author of the best-selling book *Return to the Sacred,* Executive Director of the Althea Center for Engaged Spirituality, guest on the Oprah Winfrey Show.

ꙮ

"*Jewels in the Net of the God* is a tale lived out across sacred traditions and time. It reads like an alchemical mix of mystical journey, spiritual autobiography, and love story woven through luscious lifetimes. The miraculous of the deep currents that carry us in this life swirl to the surface in each encounter, each chapter. Through this rich story these currents coax us to "meet ourselves in our own heart."

—**Tobin Hart, PhD**, university professor, author, psychologist, and consultant, interviewed by Oprah Winfrey. He is co-founder and chair of the Board of Directors of ChildSpirit Institute. His latest book is *The Four Virtues; Presence, Heart Wisdom and Creation*.

"Dr. Lorell Frysh's book is like a mysterious road map where all roads lead to a glorious meeting point that transcends time and space. A novel with both the mystery and the story to capture the reader as well as offering a guide to some of the great spiritual paths of the world. I was immersed in the characters and deeply enjoyed the inner journey."

—**Shahabuddin David Less**, meditation teacher, mystic, and Senior Teacher (Murshid) in the Sufi Order International, author of "Universal Meditations: A Program for Quieting the Mind."

Jewels in the Net of the Gods

Jewels in the Net of the Gods

A story inspired by,
and based on actual events

Lorell Frysh

Published by
Flowing Source Publishing
Boulder, CO
www.FlowingSourcePublishing.com

Book cover design by Nick Zelinger, NZ Graphics
Book interior design by Veronica Yager, YellowStudios

ISBN: 978-0-9967748-0-2
Library of Congress Control Number: 2015951617

To all who embrace the adventure of
living with a fearless spirit, open heart
and awakening consciousness

Acknowledgements

Love has shown up in my life as the greatest of gifts. It is the magic and mystery that sustains me as I encounter all the majesty and travails of what it means to be alive.

First and foremost it came in the form of my parents Joe and Zina Rosen, who fostered in me curiosity, joy and the confidence that allowed me to explore the world. It continues to show itself in the forms of my wonderful children Tamar and Daniel, their father, Henry, my son-in-law Owen, and my siblings Jonathan and Gillian, their spouses, Kim and Paul, and my niece Leigh and nephews, Gideon and Kai ~all soul mates, and fellow travellers on this life's journey who never shy away from joining me in the adventure.

I am indebted to the love and persistent caring of Rutha Rosen who has coached, cajoled and edited this project from the start. Profound thanks too to Murshid Shahabuddin David Less, Tobin Hart and Jonathan Ellerby for their inspiration, love and kind words.

To my students, Meg Collins, Jill Bosshart, Mitzi Terry, Anne Jaffe, Alice Berry, Daisy Saragoussi, Tony Bedell, Rebecca Walsh, Stephanie Moore and all my Kabbalah Experience Students who have trusted my guidance and been willing to engage the difficult journey towards self-awareness, and are a constant reminder to stay the course.

Namaste to my fellow travellers who continue to hold dear the pursuit of love, harmony and beauty, in particular Mindy Greene, Anna Less, Deborah Morin, Casey Bledsoe, Jen Baca, Ben Hummell, Laura Rose, Felipe Coquet, Jonathan and Lana Hewitt and Julian Goldstein.

For their continuing inspiration and guidance, thanks to His Holiness the Dalai Lama, Murshid Hazrat Inayat Khan, Pir Vilayat Inayat Khan, Pir Zia Inayat Khan, Swami Yogeshanada, Father Tom Francis, Mother Meera, Tom Bluewolf, Inyanga Noria, and the KoiSan peoples of the Kalahari.

Thanks too to my aid in the publishing process, Veronica Yager without whom this book would not have come into fruition.

Contents

Preface

At the very beginning of time, the great God Indra was inspired to weave a wondrous net that he stretched out infinitely in all directions across the heavens. In order to focus on its beauty, Indra set an exquisite, precious jewel in each 'eye' of the net. Sometimes Indra noticed that the net was frayed or needed repairing. Then he would have to send down his devas to help with the repairs. But most importantly, even though some jewels were flawed and most needed polishing, because he loved them so much, Indra made sure that each jewel would reflect all the other jewels for all of eternity!

From the Avataṃsaka Sūtra, 3rd C BCE

Introduction

There was something special about them right from the start....

Kundun liked to think that his auspicious birth was due to his Mother's prayers. His mother told him that when, like all devout Tibetan women, she felt ready to have a baby, she awoke early, tied her traditional striped apron over her clean dark dress and walked with firmness of purpose to her local temple to pray. Diligently she placed her flower and incense offering before the golden statue of the Buddha invoking his blessings of love and compassion for a good and easy birth. Diligently too, she turned the great red and gold prayer wheels in the temple courtyard clockwise sending her prayers upwards and outwards to the heavens.

As a practicing Buddhist Kundun's mother was aware of the bond between parents and children that precedes birth in this world. And that bond, she often told him, was acknowledged for her around the time of his conception when she began having dreams about her precious child informing her of his special characteristics. The dreams continued throughout her pregnancy and were confirmed by the unusual sight of an auspicious rainbow that filled the sky on the wonderful morning that he was born. She called him Kundun, she said, because it means 'Untouched Gold, or The Presence'.

Yes, Kundun liked to say that it was because of his mother's prayers. But that was his humility. In truth he knew it was much more than that......

ꝏ

Liora's mother told her that because she was having a difficult time conceiving, she made a special trip to Israel to visit Rachel's tomb, a place where, for centuries, Jewish women have prayed for help falling pregnant. The great Matriarch Rachel, barren for a long time, was the mother of Joseph and Benjamin who fathered two of the twelve tribes of Israel.

Like hundreds of generations of women before her, Liora's mother diligently tied a red string around the tomb seven times praying to be blessed with the gift of a child. And, as is the custom, wore it on her wrist throughout her pregnancy. And she told Liora that throughout her pregnancy she never had any doubt that she was carrying a girl. Neither was she in the least surprised when her beautiful daughter was born with golden brown eyes, a halo of copper hair and a deeply caring nature. It also did not surprise her that from her earliest days her child cared about strangers, loved to help others, and had a decided mystical bent. She named her Liora~"I have God's Light."

Pearl

(attunes to the ebb and flow of life; promotes faith, integrity, truth and loyalty.)

The last time Kundun was born it was a difficult birth. He was aware of that because during his meditations in the past few months information had started to arise about the origins of his being, and about the long and complex accumulation of impressions he carried from his many past lifetimes ~ information of great depth that defied all logic but was of the kind alluded to in the great Buddhist texts.

Shifting slightly, Kundun adjusted the maroon fabric of his monk's robe and refocused. It was 3.00 am, the hour when the veil between the spiritual world and this world is said to be thinnest. At this quiet hour many of the monks liked to meditate in their rooms, rolling gently from sleep into a sitting position on their simple small cot beds, turning their gaze inwards.

However, this chilly morning, like many lately, Kundun slipped out of his bed and walked purposefully down the draughty stone hallway, stepped into a tiny alcove and seated himself on his meditation cushion. Kundun liked alcoves. He liked the way they punctuated the hallways providing privacy and respite. Folding his legs lotus style, back straight, he let his gaze fall softly on his favorite meditation thanka ~ a beautiful 17th C painting of Chenrezig, the Bodhisattva of Compassion.

As a young Buddhist monk Kundun was well aware that there were many levels to his meditations. Viewing the thanka from the most external perspective, his artistic sensibility reveled in its golden sheen. He loved its softly faded glory and the fact that it had been used as a deepening tool for over two hundred years. He loved its depiction of the compassionate Buddha with its myriad eyes framed like a halo around its head, symbolizing the capacity to see all; and its multiple arms symbolic of helping all. He loved knowing that the monks, who had painted the thanka so long ago, did so in deep meditation imbuing it with the energy of their own awakened awareness. However, it was the eyes of the Buddha that drew him in the most. They always had.

The low light of the alcove kept the silk fabric surrounding the painting from disintegrating and the colors of the paint had softened to a buttery golden glow. It seemed to Kundun that the thanka itself emanated its own sense of compassion. Thinking about this brought him to a deeper level of his meditation. Kundun really enjoyed the deepening process.

Silently he chanted. "Om Mani Padme Om"~ I bow to the jewel in the lotus. I bow to the compassion that flowers, just as the lotus does, growing up from the muck at the bottom of the pond, from the sludge and difficulties of life. At this level of meditation Kundun could feel compassion as the very fabric of his being.

He knew that it had taken many, many lifetimes to come to this level of awareness ~ many lifetimes of suffering, many lifetimes of the Bardo states, the transitions towards Enlightenment. But he knew that suffering fostered growth and compassion for others and therefore had a great purpose in life, difficult as it was.

Kundun adjusted his cushion, took a breath and began his Tonglen practice, visualizing taking on the suffering of others as he breathed in, and sending happiness and success to all beings as he breathed out ~ sending peace to his friends and enemies alike. This ancient practice was part of a Boddhisattvic vow he had taken to extend a helping hand in leading all sentient beings as they moved towards nirvana. He vowed to help them before he dissolved into that ultimate state himself. No small vow, understanding as he did, that sentient beings are numberless.

Deepening his meditation even more, to the very heart of the inner secret knowing, Kundun sat in the profound awareness that although it is not always apparent, compassion and love are the very matrix of the ground of being, imbued in every moment. He knew that this was a very difficult paradox and a very expansive consciousness to hold. It was one he had grappled with for a long, long time ~ particularly in light of his last life, which took place during the horrors of World War II. His mind wandered for an instance, then he refocused, determined to save that memory for another time.

Today he needed to move more quickly through his meditations because he was about to take an important journey far away, to visit a Druze Sheik who lived near Mount Carmel in the north of Israel. Kundun first met the Sheik a few years earlier at the World Conference of Religions in Barcelona and felt an immediate rapport with him. During their conversation the subject of reincarnation arose, and when Kundun discovered that a quarter of the Druze community has spontaneous recall of their past lives, he was determined to find out more.

He and the Sheik also ascertained that belief in reincarnation was just one of many similarities between the esoteric knowledge of Tibetan Buddhism and the Druze religion, and both of them wished to explore those similarities in a deeper and more intimate environment. And so Kundun was invited to the Sheik's home for a visit. And now the time had finally come. He was excited at the prospect of travel, intuiting that the visit would be extremely important.

ꕥ

It was the quiet certitude of the old Greek Orthodox monk that Liora found most disconcerting. His sense of centered presence was as unnerving as the penetrating intensity of his strange dark eyes. Caught once again off-guard at their encounter, Liora noted that this was the third time she had unexpectedly come across him in just as many days, and each time something otherworldly seemed to happen.

That morning as she walked past the monastery guesthouse near the Damascus Gate in East Jerusalem, she was drawn inside as if by some mysterious force. She entered tentatively through the arched stone entrance, and found herself in a beautiful cloistered courtyard garden suffused with bushes of deep red roses. Their smell was intoxicating ~ like falling into wine, she thought smiling. She decided to spend her day in that courtyard, writing and contemplating. Small tables and chairs seemed to invite quiet time for reflection, and the guest house was happy to provide it.

Liora chose a seat off to the side of the courtyard, preferring the sense of anonymity the side seating provided. Since her difficult divorce, her life had taken such unusual and unexpected twists and turns that she wanted to write and meditate on what she now came to understand was a profound and unexpected spiritual journey. It had brought her to this point, this courtyard here, in Israel, a land holy to many but also important to her because her ancestors on her mother's side came from old Jerusalem.

Shifting her gaze downwards, Liora drew a deep breath and focused on the slowly melting sugar as it met the swirl of her hot mint tea. She thought about the first time she encountered the strange monk. It had been a busy day when she turned onto a tiny cobbled street in the Armenian quarter in old Jerusalem, drawn to the quiet after the intensity of the main thoroughfare. The sound of a cane tapping along the cobblestones seemed amplified to her, and strangely out of place. Quite suddenly she felt the hairs on her neck and arms rise a little. Turning almost involuntarily, she found herself face to face with the wizened old monk stark in his black robes.

The encounter was nothing more than an instant of a meeting. Not more than a nod of recognition and as suddenly as he was there, he was gone. The old monk's disquieting eyes were warm, somewhat familiar even, and they left Liora with the strong impression that he was able to see into the very depths of her being. Strangely, she felt as if she had somehow been contacted. There was no other way to express it. The contact felt profound; unearthly; an instant transmission and very unnerving.

And now, in the monastery courtyard, here he was again. Because he was already sitting when she arrived, Liora knew the monk had not followed her, but she felt a disconcerting sense that their brief encounters were not at all random. She forced herself to look at him. As she did he rose, nodded to her briefly and walked over, wordlessly dropping a note on her table.

Liora was thoroughly taken aback. Intrigued, she opened the envelope to find an invitation for a meeting at a Rabbi's house in one of the religious settlements on the West Bank for the next afternoon. "Welcome to the Abrahamic Reunion" it said. "Please come tomorrow to the following address……" It was a strange invitation, and she was not sure how to react. On the one hand she was a little apprehensive ~ her brief interactions with the monk were intense, and yet, like the old monk himself, she found the invitation oddly compelling.

Quartz

(reminds you of who you are, why you are here, and gives courage to take action)

Kundun began the eight-and-a-half hour taxi cab ride from Dharamsala to Delhi soon after breakfast. He knew that it would be a long flight from Delhi to Tel Aviv and was pleased to have the time to contemplate which of his many past life memories he wished to share with the Druze Sheik. He had been sharing those memories with his teacher, needing to discuss them, because as a Buddhist, he understood that although they were part of a lived experience, ultimately they were a part of Maya, the illusion of being. He did not want to hold onto past impressions that might be limiting. Lately, his memories seemed to be emerging from his deep unconscious with an insistence he found perplexing, and he was surprised by their emotional intensity. Kundun wondered why they were arising at this time in his life. His teacher encouraged him not to dismiss them but to watch them with mindfulness, allowing them place in his psyche without attachment.

Thoughtful about the process of life, Kundun recalled that some mystical traditions, the Sufis for example, suggest that the soul of the baby brings the parents together. Or perhaps, Kundun thought, we belong to a group of souls who span the dimensions of time and space, joining together to create an intricate web of love, joy and karmic lessons ~ such a powerful web that it expands the very fabric of the Universe itself. Of one thing Kundun was sure, everything is interconnected and everything is dependent on everything else. He was certain there must be a reason that in his past lives he kept coming into contact with the same souls who seemed to perform significant roles with him throughout many lifetimes.

Kundun's taxi raced down from the high mountains of Himchal Pradesh in the Western Himalayas. As the green forests gave way to the brown flatlands and they sped through countless small villages, he dropped into deep meditation. Initially his consciousness was simply at Stillpoint where he experienced a profound nothingness ~ no separation, no form, no time, no space. It had taken him many years of dedicated meditation to reach the ability to experience no mind activity at all.

But then he was flooded with memories from the very beginnings of his journey as an individuated soul. The Great Journey is what he called it. All sentient beings, he knew, take it and it involves eons of progression through differentiation and vibrational shifts. As the universe exploded out of nothing and birthed the gasses, stars and planets, it birthed the journey of what Kundun would call his individual 'soul.'

During the course of his discussions with his teacher, Kundun learned that it is necessary for the soul to forget its connection to Oneness, and to experience separation in order to learn and grow and share in the karmic lessons that life brings. This process, he understood, would take many lifetimes before his soul eventually became enlightened. Only then would it return to the great expanded consciousness of the One Being.

Kundun knew that by the time he stretched out of the warmth and security of his mother's womb gulping in air and meeting the shock of life in this world, his 'soul' had been traveling an amazing course, a course older than time itself. The physical plane, he realized, was not the beginning.

ℜ

Sitting in the shade of an olive tree in the monastery courtyard, Liora thought regretfully about the things that had gone badly in her marriage. It was fair to say that life had been good to her, so a palpable shock ran through her community when, after fifteen years, her marriage fell apart. She and her husband were, on the surface of things, a golden couple ~ wealthy, young, and vibrant. They had great kids, traveled the world, contributed to the community, helped build a school, and were building their dream house - a large Italian-inspired villa in the heart of the city, with walls the color of warm beach sand especially plastered by a group of Romanian stucco workers who knew how to create a villa that looked as if "it had been there forever like part of a ruin".

Perhaps, Liora thought regretfully, they should have recognized this "ruin" as a clue; a portent. But then there were many clues they missed. When they first walked the land ~ an unusual two acres of pristine pine, wild rhododendrons and dogwoods that skirted a little lake in the middle of the city~ they conveniently ignored the warning signs of anger and discontent that were the undercurrent of their daily lives. Liora also ignored another sign ~ one that only she could know about.

On that walk they hiked uphill for a while and at a certain point stopped to rest. Looking down just where she stopped, Liora noticed a tiny tortoise, not much bigger than her hand, its shell a beautiful mottled brown. As she stooped to look at it closely, she was taken aback by its unusual markings. There, very clearly, was the imprint of a pair of eyes staring at her, challenging her to take notice. She stood up quickly, telling herself she was imagining things, and hurriedly moved on saying nothing, pushing the incident to the back of her awareness, because she found the all-seeing eyes extremely disconcerting.

She and her husband went ahead blithely, caught in the dream of invincibility that is the drama and illusion of youth. They were proud to be the expression in their community of insouciance, a certain "je ne sais quoi" of gilded privilege. They entertained a lot. Their parties were fun, and unusual. They had an image to uphold after all. When they broke ground and laid the first blocks of the foundation of the house, they held a special ceremony to celebrate the coming creation. At the suggestion of an Indian friend of theirs, they buried a ruby, an emerald, some gold and some spices in the foundation wall, as was the custom in Southern India. It all felt very interesting, and symbolic ~ but of what they were not quite sure.

And they had failed to register that instead of taking a ritual from India, they should have focused much closer to home. Their beautiful piece of land, they later found out, was a Native

American Burial ground ~ sacred land to a people who honored the earth and the place of the ancestors in a way that they had yet to understand.

In truth, the foundation of their lives together, their marriage, was deeply fissured. And to be honest, there were warning signs from the beginning. Beginnings Liora had since learnt, are very important. They put energetic patterns in place whose tendrils reach far out into, and affect, the future. And like the blueprint for a new house, they require attention. Liora and her husband were clearly not paying attention.

The lesson was a hard one. She wished that she and her ex-husband could have honored the Native Americans on whose sacred land they had inadvertently built their house. They would have learnt a lot about foundations and grounding. She knew now that though neither sexy nor glamorous, foundations are the unseen roots that hold tenaciously to the dank, groundedness of the deep earth and draw elemental succor from hidden realms. Her foundational support, she learned, needed to be strong and fortified and made of values that are real and lasting. And it had to be flexible, pliable enough to hold fast in life's inevitable storms.

Interestingly though, Liora reflected, as a child she was very connected to the earth. She remembered one day when she was about seven years old, playing in a remote corner of her grandparents' African farm. She had followed the winged charm of a butterfly into the heart of an abandoned building and stumbled upon a tiny courtyard brimming with secret life. Red and yellow weaver birds darted industriously amongst their braided nests, geckos flitted nervously along crumbling walls, shafts of sunlight threw rainbows across the rill of an old fountain, and the whole magical world droned with myriad insects. Liora fell to her small knees in awe and gratitude. Suddenly, in that precious moment, she felt an overwhelming feeling of love for everything in her world.

Reflecting on that early sense of connectedness, and contrasting it with the disconnectedness inherent in her marriage, Liora could see why the marriage could not last. Although she'd entered into it full of hope and some good had come from it, she understood that it had to end. She recognized now that she had to learn to live in a more connected and authentic way, an important step on a spiritual journey whose trajectory she could not, at that time even begun to imagine.

Chrysocolla

(strength, balance, harmony, attunement with the earth)

As she sat immersed in the rich smells of flowers and earth in the Monastery courtyard, reminded of how she loved the nature of her childhood, Liora remembered an experience she was privileged to have in the Kalahari Desert with the Koisan Bushmen soon after her divorce.

Her trip came as an unexpected relief after a chance meeting with an ethno-musicologist who had just spent time with a small group of the indigenous nomads. Liora knew she needed something to take her away from the pain and heartache of her broken marriage, and so she convinced him to give her the contact information of the person who helped him connect with those remote Bushmen.

Not long after, Liora and some of her friends found themselves driving ten hours into the vast desert to meet one of the least accessible groups of people in the world. Her surprise, when they finally made contact, was how immediately comfortable she felt with the warmth and sweetness of the people, and the simple daily rhythm of their lives. She was surprised too at the odd sense of comfort and déjà vu she experienced in the open scrub bush, so very different from the way she grew up, and put it down to the idea that since early man came from Africa, the feeling was probably held deep in the memory bank of her blood and DNA.

But when after an incident when a young toddler fell into the fire and was badly burnt Liora, without any thought whatsoever, went straight to an aloe plant, cut open the tough stalk and applied the sap to the child's burns, she began to question where her instinctive knowledge came from. The women in the group cheered her with enthusiasm and indicated that she had done exactly as they would have done. Liora had been doing past life regression sessions for a while and decided right then to investigate whether she had ever lived a life in the desert as a Bushman.

Although it was a rather unusual thing to do, Liora had been interested in reincarnation for most of her life, and the regression sessions helped her access many past lives. Soon after her trip to the Kalahari, she went for another session, and she was not surprised to discover that she had indeed been a Bushman hunter. The knowledge made her smile, remembering the moment she and her friends parted from the Bushmen. Their leader offered her a gift of the only thing he owned ~ his wonderful buckskin hunting kit complete with digging stick, fire-making sticks, and bow and arrows. She was thrilled with his generosity, surprised at his insistence that she take it, and delighted to watch his simple practicality as he went directly to a bush and started to make another.

As they drove away from the group, their land rover bumping over the sandy earth, Liora looked back and noticed him, raised stick in hand, a message of salute from one comrade to another. It was as if he was sending her a blessing from her past, she thought, to carry forward as she moved courageously into her future….

ꝏ

Kundun was amused by the bright pink tin and tinsel framed picture of Ganesha, the elephant god, remover of obstacles, hanging from the taxi's rear view mirror. It seemed to be the only thing keeping them from careening into the local population. Kundun enjoyed the small countryside villages they passed on their way to Delhi. Life in those villages, he knew, was simple ~ difficult at times perhaps, but there was a comfort in its rhythm of daily-ness punctuated by regular festivals to honor and propitiate the gods. There was an innocence in that lifestyle that he liked ~ a sense of knowing one's place in the grander scheme of things.

Slipping back into meditative awareness, Kundun connected with the simplicity of the angelic plane, to the time when his soul was in its purest form. In the angelic plane he still felt deeply connected to the memory of Source, his vibrations were extraordinarily refined, imbued with primordial sound and suffused with light. As a ray of divine light, he experienced no sense of individual consciousness ~ only of harmonious nature. He had yet to sense any dualities such as good or bad, happiness or sadness. He was simply a pureness that reflected Divine Love, attuned to music and the workings of nature, and connected to human consciousness in a good way, often intervening by inspiring prophets, providing insight, protection and guidance for people, awakening their imagination and intuition, and accompanying their souls from one life to the next.

He recognized an innocence in his being that he carried into one of his first lifetimes, an ancient life he had lived in earliest Africa ~ a time of deep-connectedness when he was a woman named !Knomsie. The fact that he had been a woman did not surprise him. The soul, he came to know, took many forms throughout its lifetimes.

Africa: Before recorded time

As a young girl, !Knomsie often found herself peering curiously into the warm darkness of the local medicine woman's hut, intrigued by the secrets that were extracted from a toss of the bones, and fascinated by the plants and herbs the medicine woman used to heal the community. She loved the smoky dimness, and relished hearing about her future as she settled against the rounded contours of the grass walls, immersing herself in the rich smells of thatch and pounded earth. !Knomsie always remembered the time when the bones foretold of her own work with plants, and that she would be married to a strong, good man who would take care of her. To her that meant he would hunt well and provide enough meat for the family. She could not expect more.

Most of the time, her people, the Khoisan Bushmen, lived without shelter, out in the open, in harmony with the earth and the harsh elements of the Kalahari Desert. They did not need much, and they did not own much: bows and arrows for some; tortoise shell medicine containers for others; digging and fire sticks, and the occasional ostrich shell necklace. !Knomsie always felt that her life was satisfying and good.

Many, many, moons passed, until her last difficult night with her man. As usual, the shift from the heat of the day was swift and dramatic. It took a short 20 minutes for the searing orange ball of the sun to sink below the horizon, and suddenly the world was plunged into a profound inky blackness broken only by the pale light of the stars and the moon, which never felt more welcome.

!Knomsie and her family moved closer into the tightly knit circle of light and warmth of the fire that represented safety in the vast expanse of shadow and predator that comprise the nighttime experience of the Kalahari Desert. As they settled happily, their chatter dying off slowly and sleepily, they drifted into the semi-dream, semi-awake-ness that is the way of the desert dweller. A deep peace defined their circle.

!Komsie however, was not sleeping. She was thinking about the time when she first met her strong hunter that beautiful morning so long ago, when she was out in the scrub-bush digging for plants. It had been an auspicious year, just after the unusual great rains, and the ground was covered in a carpet of tiny yellow and white flowers. The air was humming with insects. Birds wheeled happily in the sky, and everything was rich and sweet.

!Komsie had just finished digging up a giant tuber whose juice she planned to use to rub her skin clean when she felt a shadow fall across her path. Startled, she looked up to see his outstretched hand offering her an unexpected gift ~ a beautiful copper-hued butterfly, the same color as his warm, deeply focused eyes. She was especially touched that he had refrained from darting her in the buttocks with his tiny courting arrow, as was the usual way of signaling interest to young maidens.

Although he was somewhat a stranger, he was not completely unfamiliar. He came from a neighboring family group and she had spied him playing with her brothers on occasion. From behind the discreet security of a dense scrub bush, she'd watched as the young men sharpened their sticks, and sent them flying spear-like far into the surrounding bush. !Knomsie was impressed at how fast and far his stick would fly, and how he always won the game. But what impressed her most was that he was always helpful and quick to laugh.

After they committed to each other, the fluidity of their lives continued seamlessly. For the Khoisan people that meant moving with what the earth and the universe provided. As a community they valued co-operation, sharing, caring, simplicity, laughter, an essential creativity and a powerful resilience. They made music and love together, enjoyed decorating their utensils with crude pictures of the animals they encountered, and danced and sang together. Because their lives depended on it, they honored what they knew to be important.

!Knomsie remembered well the coming of her oldest child. The morning started out chilly, the bush just beginning to wake, when she felt the first sharp pains. Pale tendrils of dawning light caught the treetops and slowly warmed the ground. Insects began to buzz, birds shook themselves in the half-light, grazing herds, alert and tentative, made their cautious way to waterholes. Saying nothing, when the pains became very intense she left the camp quietly and made her way to the little hollow she had prepared behind a termite mound. Private and discreet she squatted alone in the dust.

The first hour of her labor between the growing pains was spent appreciating little things ~ stick insects that blended with the brown earth, flashes of turquoise as the lilac breasted rollers lifted into the air, guinea fowl darting across rutted ground. She focused on the spoor and buck droppings in her immediate environment. They reminded her of her strong husband and his prowess at hunting, but also she thought shyly, of their lovemaking. She was captivated too by the smell of dust, wild sage and the potato bush with its distinctive odor of breast milk.

For hours !Knomsie focused on anything and everything to distract her from the pains that rocked her insides. She noticed with heightened sensitivity the white and purple wild flowers scattered between the grass, and the enormous gossamer spider's webs spanning the distance between tree branches. She thought of the animals in whose presence her man spent his days ~ herds of grazing impala, giraffe, zebra, wildebeest, and majestic kudu that stared anxiously at him from behind trees before taking off in the fretful gallop, indicative of members of the lower levels of the food chain.

As she dropped her baby from her tired body, troops of baboon shouted a warning from the safety of treetops. The sudden crack of a tree branch alerted her to elephant, and amazingly she found herself surrounded by a herd of mothers with their babies. Keeping a respectful distance, they had watched her birthing process in silent protective arrangement ~ mothers in front, babies securely behind; except for the imperative of one newborn taking succor from the powerful body of its mother, the blood of birth still drying on its little legs.

Awed, !Knomsie looked deeply into the eyes of her little one, remembering that a couple of days earlier she chanced upon a butterfly emerging from its chrysalis, its soft dewy clump of wings slowly unfurling and warming in the sunlight. The miracle of flight, when it finally came, was no less breathtaking, no less poignant, and no less powerful than the miracle surrounding her the morning when she brought her own child into the world.

Later that year when out collecting aloe juice for soothing wounds, she caught the sharp, pungent smell of blood hanging in the afternoon air. She had only to follow the circling vultures to meet again the cycle of life. Silver-backed jackals pacing the area were a sure sign that a kill was near. And then she was almost upon it ~ a pride of lion dozing lazily, the half-eaten carcass of their latest meal awaiting further attention. Lion cubs, endearing in their kittenish playfulness, stumbled over their mother's bloated stomach, stopping every now and then to suck from swollen teats. !Knomsie always marveled at the cycle of life.

And now in the cold of his last night she lay next to her man, open to the significance of the coming dawn. He had grown old and tired, her brave hunter, and on his last hunt he had injured himself badly. No amount of aloe juice would heal that wound. They consulted with the medicine healer who upon shaking the bones from his old skin bag read the end of his days and entreated him to make peace with himself and his family ~ to recognize again the miracle of blood and milk, birth and death; the fine balance in the way life creates itself, supports itself, destroys itself, creates itself, in its ongoing process. Together they sat and acknowledged with wonder how the great sweep of nature had pulled them together and how they were now to say their goodbyes.

The next morning, leaving him under a tree with a little food, an ostrich egg filled with water and the knowledge that he had lived a good life, !Knomsie knew it would not be too long before the lions or hyenas came for him. She knew too that he would be ready when it happened, just as he had known it was in the order of things when he spoke to the plants, and when he had asked permission from the animals, who agreed to feed his family with their meat. He was aware, as the animals were, of his place in the cycle of things, and he understood his position now. !Knomsie was proud of him ~ her brave hunter who knew equally well how to live, and how to die.

After one last glancing exchange !Knomsie turned resolutely away and did not look back, walking forthrightly north with her family, following the migration of the birds.

Onyx

(promotes self-control, assists in grieving, breaks down barriers that hold one back)

Liora ordered breakfast and was glad when it arrived in a simple carved wooden bowl. Cupping her hands around the silky smoothness of the bowl, she felt a connection to decades of monks silently communing with their morning porridge. Liora loved bowls. Bowls and boxes. She loved the inner-ness of them ~ their capacity to hold both the mundane and the precious. Once during a past life regression session she discovered that she had taught herself to make bowls from the soft wood of fallen logs……

ཀ྅

Kundun tried to return to his meditation, but the dusty chaos of the villages kept intruding on his consciousness. He could no longer connect with the angelic plane. Instead, he felt himself drawn to the astral plane where he experienced himself becoming denser, more differentiated and more contracted. He felt a piercing pain as if an aspect of himself had splintered off and shifted dimensions. And he had a strange sensation of loss and longing ~ a feeling he recognized he would carry with him for the rest of time.

As his awareness moved deeper onto the astral plane, Kundun felt himself gather the vibrations of color and dimension. His mind became more captive, and he found that he began to desire knowledge and understanding. He forgot his angelic consciousness and became attracted to all that is definable ~ to art, mathematics, dreams, deep unconscious archetypal memories, stories and forms.

Kundun knew it was to one of the numerous realms of the astral plane, Bardo, Tibetan Buddhists call it, that his soul would return between lifetimes. And it was here that he gained the vibrational gravity which pulled him towards his physical incarnations, towards his first parents, his life's lessons, his growth and his potential on the earth plane.

He became aware that initially he experienced resistance before he came to the earth plane. Somehow, he intuited that life on earth could be very intense. But it was on earth that he would be tempered and polished, and would learn to embrace imperfection and limitation. And then suddenly, and painfully, he had a memory of the lifetime when he experienced his first great loss....

France: Before recorded time

It was the time just after the large rains. The air was cooler now and the leaves were falling lifeless off the trees creating heaps of crunching, yellow carpet underfoot. Animals were preparing for the great sleep and the boy and his mother were searching for a new home. They had become used to this particular cave, liking the way it sheltered them from the summer's heat, and more particularly for the fact that its depth protected them from roaming savage ones ~ strange men looking for women, and animals in search of meat. However, recently they had heard wild brown bears near the entrance to the cave and it no longer felt safe to remain there.

The boy was sad to leave. He enjoyed exploring deep into the darkness of the cave and had found an open place where his song resonated best off the stone walls, echoing back, calling and calling, as if from the very depths of the earth. He delighted in finding his voice and playing with the rhythms he created. After a long day foraging, he and his mother loved to spend time calling to the rocks and reveling in their answers. It was also to this part of the cave that he carried the fire so he could see where to mark the walls with the red ochre clay he found near the riverbed. He was particularly proud of the way he portrayed the deer he was learning to spear on his daily hunting expeditions.

The boy was especially delighted his mother allowed him to go out on his own now even though his body had not yet filled out. It was a long time, several seasons of rain, since the powerful man had been around, and they were both getting tired of eating only the fruits and herbs they gathered daily from the surrounding countryside. Occasionally they would connect with others who came into the area, and if there were other women with them, they would share food together. But mainly it was just the two of them. It was a solitary life, in which they had learned to trust and care for each other.

Readying for the move, they gathered up their meager belongings. The boy carried his spear proudly, together with his stone axe. The woman took the bowls she had fashioned from the softer wood she found from a fallen tree. She had delighted in gouging them into shape with her flint-stone arrowheads, and although they were quite heavy, and carrying them left her no free hands, they were her prize possessions and were coming with her.

She hoped too that they would find a safe place in the near vicinity with similar vegetation, because she had just begun to notice that certain of the plants she harvested had predictable results when taken in just the right way. She crushed and ground the plants in her bowls, and for this they had precious value for her.

They had just stepped out of the cave when the mother slipped on the slick leaves left behind by the night rain. In horror the boy watched, as hands full, she stumbled and hit her head against the rock at the mouth of the cave. She was a strong woman, lithe and able-bodied, but as the boy found out, it was impossible to defend ones-self against the unforgiving granite. Suddenly a new-found depth of feeling and anguish rose in his small heart as he watched his mother's eyes slip back into their sockets and disappear ~ those eyes that had watched him lovingly as he nursed, and followed him anxiously when he roamed a little too far from the cave.

Grief hit the boy hard. The dark rains seemed to have inhabited his small body, flooding him with thunder and lightning. With great difficulty he dragged his mother's lifeless body to the side of the river where the earth was less dense. Instinctively he dug a shallow grave for her. Laying her tenderly into the ground, he carefully placed her precious bowls on top of her, sobbing as he filled them with plants. Then, covering her with the red soil, he reverently placed a few sprigs of her favorite herbs, rosemary and sage, ceremoniously on top of the earth mound.

Mute with grief he sat long hours watching the water until the light cast elongated shadows across the stream, and the river rocks began to lose their definition in the fading light. He rose slowly, picking up his spear, raised it in his left hand in an unconscious gesture of salute, and pressed his right hand tightly against his heart.

Then he turned and walked purposefully down the darkening path.

Amethyst

(beneficial in areas of spirituality and justice, protects travelers)

Sweet fresh mint steeped in hot water with honey, a specialty of the monastery, the monks informed her. Liora smiled. On her way to Israel this trip, she stopped in Egypt where she was introduced to mint tea steeped in hot water. She found it refreshing, especially in the heat of the day.

Liora went to Egypt at the request of her Sufi teacher, who, upon hearing that she was going to be in the Middle East, asked her to please go there to meet with Mohammed. Odd requests to stretch oneself by doing things out of the ordinary, or by meeting certain unusual people, are often part of the Sufi teaching path, and so she went, not at all unwillingly, because she had always been fascinated by the pyramids and temples of ancient Egypt.

Liora loved Cairo. She especially loved the older part of the city where she spent hours in the Egyptian Museum, completely absorbed by the exhibitions of jewelry and artifacts from the

Middle Kingdom. She sat meditating for one whole morning in the heart of the queen's chamber in the largest of the pyramids at Giza, absorbed in the architecture and the construction of shafts of air and light that threw interesting oblique shadows against the walls of the inner chamber. It was there in the familiar half-light she suddenly remembered her past life as an architect during the time of the pharaohs.

But all the while she spent in the city she kept feeling a strong hankering to be out in the desert ~ so much so that it had begun to feel like an obsession. So she asked Mohammed, the friend of her Sufi teacher, to please help her to get out into in the Sinai, into that vast expanse of sand and rock that borders the intensely blue Mediterranean Sea.

And soon she found herself, as the heat of the day started its steep uphill climb to a searing 126 degrees F, negotiating the roll and lurch that is the uncomfortable gait of the camel. It took Liora about two hours before she relaxed into the see-saw motion; before she surrendered enough to realize that if she was to survive this ambitious trip, she was going to have to in some way, become the camel herself.

There are many forms of Mohammed that one meets in Egypt, some more esoteric, some less so. On the Sinai desert part of her trip, the Mohammed Liora encountered came in the form of a young Bedouin who was doing a favor for the Mohammed friend of her Sufi teacher, after her fervent request to "take this crazy woman on a camel trip into the desert and show her what she thinks she needs to find there." Liora was not sure why, but the camel trip felt very important. It had elements of her genetic history to it, of that she was sure, but it also had the lure of the open sky, the sand, sun, and stars, and most of all the silence she seemed to be craving.

They set off together into that vast monotonous emptiness, hearts to the wind, open to the messages of the eternal. Out there they could taste the silence. It flowed over and through them until they disappeared into it and into an indescribable feeling of their own utter smallness and unimportance. And so they rode on.

After a few hours, they stopped at a wadi, a dry river-bed, for the inevitable pot of mint tea that Liora found out, was the elixir and conduit of hospitality in that part of the world. Tentatively Liora asked her host, who right then was also her savior since without him she truly would have become an insignificant part of the desert dust, what he did when he was not leading strange women out into the middle of nowhere. He smiled gently and told her that he was a healer. And so their talk turned to healing, since this was her profession too. They talked quietly of ways and methods, of mystery schools and ancient knowledge, until again the silence enveloped them. Consumed by it, they continued quietly on their way.

After a great deal of time, out in the middle of that seemingly interminable sea of undulating sand, loomed the unexpected yet comforting and welcome sight of an ancient temple. Tall worn pillars stood proud against the open sky. The subtle, precise intricacy of the ancient mosaic floor was a sight for weary eyes. The surety of that un-shifting ground and the mysteriously etched columns that have stood the test of weathering and centuries had as it turned out, beckoned others as well. There they encountered a small group of Bedouin who had also chosen the stone pillars as their bulwark against the gathering night.

Liora could have been concerned in the presence of those black-robed strangers, strong men who live with the fierceness inherent to such a harsh land, but she was not. Conversation, she found, turns naturally to depth and the sacred in the face of such remote history and timelessness. Slouching against the strength of those ancient columns they talked of other pillars ~ the pillars most sacred to her group of fellow travelers ~ the five pillars that are the cornerstone of their Muslim faith, and on which they base the truth of their lives: creed, prayer, fasting, charity and pilgrimage.

They talked about who among them had been on the long rewarding Hajj to Mecca; who was still saving for that arduous trip; and most particularly, how they were working on their own inner Hajj ~ that most difficult pilgrimage to conquer their nafs or inner demons, those unexamined fear impulses that serve to keep one separate from oneself and others. And as they talked, they felt the sacred breath of Allah blow through them with the rise and fall of their conversation. Through it all they discovered a deep sense of peace and connectivity that enveloped their motley group of travelers and bound them together.

So when the time came to part, and they said their final goodbyes, they took a moment to acknowledge and recognize the miracle of healing that had taken place in the desert between Jewess and Muslim, male and female. They noted with genuine warmth, that out there, none of those things mattered. As they bade each other Shalom/Salaam, Liora knew why she felt such a sense of the imperative about the trip. They, in their own small way, were contributing to a healing in the world. And for that they needed to lean on the surety of their own inner pillars ~ those magnificent structures of trust, faith and strength that support the edifices and fabric of their lives.

Alhamdulillah, Liora thought as they parted ways, Mohammad would be have been pleased!

ഗ

After driving for hours in silence, the taxi driver noticed that Kundun was not longer meditating. He was curious about the Buddhist monk who could be so quiet for so long, and began asking him questions about his path. It began many, many lifetimes ago, Kundun answered, long before he came into a human body. The taxi driver was interested but he really liked it when Kundun told him more about his past human lives. The driver especially wanted to know when the monk first held a position as a spiritual leader. Kundun smiled shyly. "It was as priestess in ancient Egypt", he said "in a time of great crisis……..

Egypt: 18th Dynasty BCE

Iset walked urgently down the long white corridor towards the temple. She was agitated because as a priestess, she was very aware of the significance of sacred numerology and its connection to one's life…she was perturbed by the fact that in the past few days she had experienced three very disturbing incidents. Iset knew the importance of the Law of Threes. Her mind kept reviewing the incidents and she felt very unsettled.

Firstly, she noted, she had recently fallen in love ~ with Ineni, the court architect. She remembered when she first met him on the day he visited the temple in order to oversee the extensive renovations. He carried himself with the all the authority of power and wealth, and Iset was intrigued. Although, she had to admit to herself, it was the seductive beauty of his golden brown eyes that initially captured her attention.

And she also found herself delighted and affirmed by his response to her request for a special musical chamber in the temple. She was very happy that he immediately suggested placing the chamber in the deepest inner recesses of the Temple so that the priestesses could sing to the gods. This made such a strong impression on her because she heard the voice of the gods in the nuances of the echoes to her songs, and most of the builders could not begin to understand why it made a difference where the chamber was situated. Iset also delighted in the fact that Ineni really understood how to use sacred geometry, numerology, the mathematics of nature, and the celestial motions of the planets in his plans for the temple. She admired his capacity to join together the heavens and the earth in his design.

Soon they became lovers, and it was exceptionally pleasing to them that afternoons spent lovemaking included avid discussions about the magical properties of specific stone and metal building materials. They spent hours discussing how to focus the light of the sun god so that the temple would be ablaze with magic and mystery at certain times of the day, and at specific times of the year.

As for Ineni, she knew he found her the very embodiment of the sacred goddess. But their liaison was becoming a problem. The power of their connection was obvious to all who saw them ~ it was clear their attraction went beyond the physical and that they understood and enjoyed each other on a more profound level. That was a problem because his wife, never able to capture his interest for very long, was upset and was causing trouble at court. And this was adding to Pharaoh Thutmose's irritation.

The second disturbing incident Iset had to deal with was that she had been spotted talking to the upstart Hebrew, Moses, by one of the handmaidens who served Ineni's wife. The conversation was innocent enough and transpired when she saw him walking down a side street near the palace. She was intrigued by what she had heard about his experience in the desert and stopped to ask him about it.

Ever since Moses had returned from Midian things had been strange. It was said that his courage came from an encounter he had with a voice in the heart of a burning bush. The encounter gave him the strength to return to the Pharaoh and audaciously demand that he allow his people to leave the country. After Pharaoh Thuthmose refused, all sorts of difficulties ensued ~ curses and plagues. The court was enveloped with the fear of sorcery, and the Pharaoh was determined to stamp it out.

As one of the trusted temple priestesses, the health and continuity of the whole community was dependent on how she interceded and communicated with the gods, on behalf of the Pharaoh. As innocent as her conversation was, speaking to someone such as Moses whose actions were negatively impacting the kingdom would be seen as a villainous and traitorous act.

Iset was heavy hearted. She had always been loyal to the Pharaoh, but the times were extremely challenging and people were highly suspicious. The Hebrews were increasing in population and Pharaoh Thuthmose was also worried that they might help Egypt's enemies. The last thing Iset needed was to be perceived as helping potential enemies.

To compound matters, the third thing Iset had to deal with was a very disturbing dream from the previous night. As a priestess, she took dreams very seriously, regularly interpreting them for others. She knew that when the call came from the underworld, you dare not ignore its message. As a follower of the gods Sekhemet and Tehuti, she was taught how to commune with them and connect to her inner wisdom. And that was what she had to do now. She had to ascertain the true meaning of her unnerving dream.

Arriving at the temple, Iset was relieved to find that she was alone. She was in no mood to talk to anyone or to explain her reasons for being there so late. Hurriedly she made her way to the purification area, anxious to complete this first necessary part of the ritual. When she reached the bathing pool she quickly removed her heavy gold and lapis lazuli necklace, tossing it carelessly on a chair. Grimacing ruefully at the row of ankhs, the symbol of life, carved into the chair's wooden backrest, she was concerned about how life would treat her now.

Hastily she kicked off her braided papyrus sandals, symbols of her priestly caste, and removed her coin-decorated wig, dropping it and her flaxen robe onto the marble floor. Then she slipped naked into the oil-and-fruit infused waters in order to purify herself, before she was ready to talk with the gods. Usually Iset loved this part of the sacred ceremony. But tonight was different. She did not have time to soak or dally.

After bathing for the minimum amount of time possible, she dressed quickly, lit a candle to illuminate the path between the rows of papyrus and lotus-shaped columns, and made her way to the inner chamber near the back of the temple. Only the priestesses were allowed in this part of the temple because it was here that the divine presence manifested most strongly.

Tenderly she removed the golden statue of her namesake goddess Iset from its bark shrine. Singing hymns of praise, her sweet voice belying her fears about the meaning of her dream, she painstakingly honored and anointed the statue with oil and paint. And after offering the obligatory incense, fruit, meats and honey, she quietly entered the trance required to receive the communication that would decipher her dream.

The dream images were clear. Iset saw herself sitting down at a carved stone writing table jotting a note on a piece of old parchment. Then she removed her clothes, smeared fat all over her naked body, stared long and hard at her image in a highly polished hand mirror, and turning her back on the chamber, picked up a bow and arrow and walked down to the river where she plunged headlong into the icy cold water.

Iset shivered. Instantly the meaning of her dream became crystal clear to her. In fact, she noted with consternation, she'd been so upset by her recent circumstances, she'd failed to notice that every image in her dream had a traditional meaning. Deciphering it put it all in perspective ~ her destiny was glaringly obvious. However, just to make sure, she went through the dream images one-by-one, making mental notes as she did.

She recognized that in her dream, in order to bring her misdeeds to light, she wrote them down on a piece of parchment. She knew that by taking off her clothes she had metaphorically let go of her outer garments, or the outer framework of her life, and that taking a deep hard look at herself in the mirror meant facing the truth of her life. How often, she sighed, had she told people that smearing fat on their bodies meant that their people would be taken away from them. And now it was her turn to acknowledge that difficult truth.

She felt the resistance and fear in her heart, but the dream was clear. She would have to turn away from all she knew and seek a new life. She would have to take up the metaphorical bow and arrow that indicated the possibility of shooting at a new mark, a new way of living. And of course that would involve plunging into the stark cold waters of reality and cleansing herself of everything she knew.

And because Iset was true to her work, and because she held Ineni in too high esteem to be willing to ruin his life and his work, she understood with a heavy heart that she would have to become the sacrificial lamb. She would have to leave everything behind, taking with her only her courage and her wisdom.

As the first pale glow of the new morning rose with the mist, Iset prayed her last prayer in the Dream Temple of the Great Mother. "Come to me, come to me, O my mother Iset! "she cried, "Behold, I am seeing things which are far from my dwelling place!"

Then covering her head, she slipped silently out of the temple and joined the Hebrews on their way to the Sea of Reeds. Once the miracle of the crossing found her safe on the other side of the waters, she turned away from the Hebrews as they walked northwards, and navigating by the stars, Iset started the long hard journey eastwards across the rolling sands to meet the dawn of her new life.

Tiger's Eye

(focus, protection, enhances connection, insight)

A large monarch butterfly caught Liora's eye as it flitted amongst the flowers in the cloistered courtyard. Liora mulled over the fact that her spiritual journey felt much like that butterfly, gaining insight here and wisdom there from all the various experiences and teachers she had encountered on her journeys around the world. And of course she could not ignore the profundity of her mystical experiences either.

She thought about her first trip to Israel when she was just seventeen. The trip was a gift marking the end of her high school years. Graduation gifts were a common ritual amongst her social set, and many of her friends chose jewelry. She lived, after all, in a country known for mining gold and diamonds, and jewels were an important part of any self-respecting girl's wardrobe. Yet for her, these treasures seemed a little hollow. Liora was very interested in treasure to be sure, but she intuited even then that what she craved was a treasure much greater than the beautiful trinkets chosen by her friends. Besides, she wanted to travel. "I have gypsy blood," she would tell her friends. Somewhere deep inside her, for reasons unbeknownst to her, she had always felt the stirring of the open road.

She chose as her gift tickets to London, France and Israel. Her grandparents had traveled from the Levant to Africa in the early 20th century in order to seek their fortunes. Perhaps, she mused, it was from them that she had inherited her love of travel. Family lore told of her grandfather stowing away on a ship when he was sixteen in order to escape conscription into the Turkish army. His ship landed in Cape Town and he stepped onto the docks a free man excited to make his way in a strange new world. Liora recognized that she carried those genes ~ the need for freedom and the courage to take risks.

She was not really sure why she chose to go to England and France, but once there she found that she "knew" her way around the French streets, and that she "knew" both the French and English country sides. She experienced a strong sense of déjà vu in those places, but it was in Israel at Rachel's Tomb that her spiritual curiosity was really awakened.

Liora had always wanted to visit the place where her mother's prayers had been answered. It was her uncle, who was one of the soldiers who liberated Jerusalem during the 1967 war, who took her to visit Rachel's Tomb. His memories, understandably, were too horrific and painful to talk about, but there was one memory, one moment, that remained with him as an oasis amongst the brutalities of that war. And he really wanted to share it with her.

The beautiful garden of the "Monastery of Silence", the old Latrun Monastery, established by French, German and Flemish Trappist monks in 1890, is situated on the old Tel Aviv/

Jerusalem road. The monks who live there are an order of Cistercians who live mainly in silence, speaking only in prayer and when deemed absolutely necessary. During the Six Day War, the monastery was briefly taken over by the Israeli Defense Force facilitating the reopening of the road to Jerusalem and making it safe for travel. Her uncle had found a moment of solace in the beautiful garden of the monastery and wanted to share its beauty with her.

On their way to the monastery they stopped on the outskirts of Bethlehem at Rachel's Tomb, that ancient place considered to be the third holiest site in Judaism where Jewish tradition has it that the Matriarch Rachel weeps for her children. Devout Jews believe that when the Jews were sent into exile after the destruction of the Temple, Rachel wept as they passed by her grave.

Liora was intrigued by the small domed building constructed around 1620 by the Ottoman Turks, to cover and protect the tomb. Walking around the building's honey colored stones, she counted the eleven stones on the rock tomb, one for each of the eleven sons of Jacob who were alive when Rachel died. Entering softly, Liora initially thought she was alone in the quiet of the tomb, but after a while she heard a soft shuffle and noticed an old woman dressed all in black, slowly and methodically lighting candles along a rock ledge at the back of the tomb.

Drawn to her, Liora moved closer, picking up a taper to light candles herself. Glancing over at the woman, Liora caught her breath. There was something in the demeanor of the woman and her ancient, craggy face that made Liora pay attention. Slowly the woman turned and reached out for her hands, taking them in her own as she searched Liora's face as if looking for a sign.

In the hushed darkness the woman's ancient voice whispered, "Just remember who you are my child. Someone a longer time ago than you can remember told you that you are made of love." The old woman's eyes glittered. Somewhere deep inside Liora felt as if she knew those words, and was being reminded of them yet again. "This knowledge should guide your life", the old woman whispered. "You will find it in the secret teachings of the Hindu Yogis, the Jewish Kabbalists, the Naqushbandi Sufis, and all others who study the sacred patterns of the Divine Mystery." Liora shivered. She knew then that she would not rest until she had found those secret teachings. And she became instantly aware that those teachings were the gift she really desired.

As the conversation drew to a close, the old woman gathered Liora into her arms. She suggested that Liora visit the Cave of Machpelah, the burial place of her ancestors Abraham, Isaac, Jacob, Sarah, Rebecca, and Leah, and also visit the tomb of Zechariah in the rock caves at the bottom of the Mount of Olives. "The burial caves in the mount," she said softly, "were for the rich of Jerusalem and its priests towards the end of the Second Temple Period, and you will recognize them because you have been there before."

And then quite suddenly, as if by magic, the old woman simply disappeared. Astonished, Liora found herself alone, holding nothing but air, not sure what had just happened to her. Yet despite the bizarreness of the experience, she was left with a glowing sense of happiness, and the residual surety that her life seemed to be part of a grand design to which she needed to be open and receptive, even when she did not understand it all.

She shared her strange experience with her uncle. He nodded silently as if not really surprised, but said nothing. Evening was drawing close, and as they drove to the monastery they shuddered at the painful reminders of the horrors of war, the shadowy skeletons of burnt-out half-tracks and tanks, ghostly in the gathering darkness.

It was late when they turned into the beautiful monastery grounds, the moon casting a silvery glow over the imposing stone building, its vineyards and olive groves. A palpable hush enveloped the monastery contributing to an uncomfortable feeling that they were trespassing on hallowed ground. Their discomfort increased when the dark hooded figure of a monk stepped silently out of the shadows, beckoning them to follow him.

The monk led them up a cold external staircase, and ushered them into the choir loft just in time for the Christmas Midnight Mass. All the pent-up passion of a life filled with a deep inner connection to silence was releasing itself in that moment, in a devotion of Gregorian chants. The heavenly music echoed through the Gothic rafters filling the vast dark space, as rows of monks made their solemn procession through the church each carrying tall white candles, their flames suffusing the church with an ethereal glow.

In that beautiful chapel they were as far as one could imagine from the flavor of Jesus' Middle East, but Midnight Mass celebrated with the spiritual devotion of a community whose existence is spent contemplating the message of Christ, brought to the Christmas story a whole new meaning of miracle.

It was a wonderful place to integrate the strange encounter Liora had experienced a few hours earlier.

After the service, in a quiet mood of reminiscence, her uncle finally spoke. He told her about an elderly woman who would mysteriously appear on the side of the road near Rachel's Tomb during the Six Day War, and who would direct the soldiers away from land mines. After negotiating their hazardous way, the soldiers would look back but see nobody there. And when they sought to thank her, they never could find any trace of her. Given her own very strange experience in the tomb, Liora felt somehow validated.

She did not have time to heed the old woman's direction to visit the tomb of Zachariah at the base of the Mount of Olives on that trip, but on her current trip she finally entered the caves from the Kidron Valley on the side invisible to the city. Once inside, she was flooded with visions of having walked the narrow passage-ways centuries before ~ not alone, but with a group of women, disciples of Yeshua, hurrying through the caves on a very important mission……

༄

The taxi driver asked Kundun whether this was his first trip to the Holy Land. His wife, he said, was a Christian from Goa, and had always wanted to go to Jerusalem. She'd told him that Jesus had spent time in India after his crucifixion, and he said, he would love to tell her what a Holy man would say about that.

Kundun smiled. He loved the enthusiasm and devotion of his driver and his open simplicity, and was happy to tell him that, yes indeed, there were records at a monastery not far from his own dating back to the time of Christ, which mentioned a teacher and Holy man from the Middle East. The Indians, he said, called the man Isa, and he fitted the descriptions and stories of Christ. What he did not tell the taxi driver was the part he had played in the story as a Bedouin woman named Amina…

Judea: 34 AD

Amina sighed, lifting her heavy earthenware water jug from the well and placing it firmly on her shoulder. Betrayal was everywhere, a slashed wound across the very heart of the country, and because this was no ordinary day, she had a lot to do before the evening came. Making her way resolutely towards her tent, she was glad for the sanctuary it provided. Typical Bedouin tents with their simple dark cloth covering were not considered very interesting or important to the ruling Roman authorities. She needed secrecy on this of all days since she had much to prepare.

It was because of her reputation as a healer and by recommendation of Joanna, the wife of Chuza who managed the household of Herod Antipas, that the women had come to her, hurried and fearful of being caught. The Jewish preacher and miracle worker had been brought to trial and it had not gone well. Amina thought about him as she prepared her basket of herbs, poultices and spices.

It was in Jerusalem that she had briefly met him, at the house of his mother Mariam, a good woman, renowned for her generosity, kindness to strangers and excellent cooking. Amina and her caravan had recently arrived from across the Sahel after a long, arduous journey ~ months navigating the unending dunes, laden with spices from the east and salt from the south. She knew the Jewish women needed her goods to kosher their food. They were good customers, who paid well and promptly, and besides, Passover was almost upon them and the women were very busy with food preparation.

Making her way through the narrow limestone streets, Amina soon found the house of Joseph and Mariam. She was intrigued by the stories she had heard of their son, the young teacher, a fierce opponent of the corruption of the Sanhedrin. She also heard of whispers of miracles, great healing powers and of words that seemed to carry the music of the heavens. Amina was overwhelmed when, rounding the corner of the narrow ally, she all but bumped into him. She felt his presence like a bolt of electricity and was shocked when his glance met hers. It was just a glance, but it pierced her soul and in it she felt the shiver of destiny. It was but a brief moment, and then he was gone.

Amina was a little nervous as she made her way to Mariam's kitchen where the community women were busy with their cooking. They conducted their business like women have done through the ages. Interwoven with the heat of price haggling, they discussed children, family and local gossip, and exchanged recipes ~ lamb stewed with rosemary and olives, fish cooked with figs and honey, meat and pine nut stuffed grape leaves, and the making of grape wine and pomegranate juice.

And because it was her passion, Amina shared her knowledge of herbs she used for healing, the secrets of the stars and other knowledge that she had gathered in her encounters with the Zoroastrian Magi far away to the East, on her caravan journeys across the vast desert sands. She told the women about the eternal flame the Magi have kept alight from the beginning of time, and about their strict moral code. The women were intrigued, commenting that they too had an eternal flame in front of the Holy Ark that held the Torah in the Temple. They were fascinated by the similarities to their moral and ethical codes. It was these tales that would prompt them to come looking for her tent in their time of need.

After the Passover meal, Amina bumped into Joanna in the spice market. Joanna was full of stories of the dinner, recounting the beautiful way in which the teacher led the meal. Amina enjoyed hearing the story told as tradition required, of the Hebrews' flight out of Egypt to freedom in the Promised Land. She especially liked it because the route was one she knew well. She was always amused that it took the ancient Hebrews so long to navigate the desert.

But most interesting to her was the esoteric meaning the teacher gave to the traditional story. He explained that hidden in the story lay a secret meaning ~ the story, he said, could be understood as a metaphor for the journey of the soul. He explained that the word for Egypt in Hebrew, Mitzraim, meant the place of the foreigner, and could refer to that which is foreign in us, our self-imposed limitations foreign to the freedom of our souls. The Passover story, he explained, is really a story about the opportunity to move away from limitation into a lifestyle where God consciousness rules ~ that, he taught, is the Promised Land, the land of the Messiah, the enlightened state. Amina was fascinated by his interpretation. It felt very inspired and somehow very right to her.

But now, the Sabbath was coming and they had to make haste. Their beloved teacher had been tried and punished as a blasphemer. At the end of his day of agony, the authorities took him down limp from his travail on the cross, wrapped him in linen and placed him in the empty tomb, a final gift from one of the few members of the Sanhedrin who admired him. Then the authorities rolled the great stone over the mouth of the tomb sealing him in forever, or so they thought. Joanna arrived soon after, with some of his female disciples, begging Amina to help them by using her healing knowledge to try and resuscitate him.

Amina and the small group of women passed silently through the city, invisible in the cloak of anonymity that is the gift of all people on the fringes of society. They walked quickly down a small side street, the magnificence of the Temple complex gleaming in the distance. They crossed quietly through the small garden of Gat Shemen with its gnarled olive trees, over the hill of the Mount of Olives to the Kidron Valley, an area hidden from the city, near the tomb of Zachariah. There, slipping into a secret crevice in the hillside, they entered the interior of the tombs.

It was cold in the tombs. Carved from the interior of the hillside, the dry dark earth held centuries of bones. Although they were not her own people, Amina respected the ancestors of the Jews and silently asked for their help in her work. She and the women hurried along, a pressing need to get to him quickly, their way made safe by their small oil lamps. When they finally entered the tomb where he lay, it was to find his body cold, his spirit already slipping into other realms.

Honoring the Sabbath and Amina's wisdom, the women watched as she worked quickly, applying her plants and poultices to his wounds, breathing her incantations and prayers, entreating him to remain on the Earth, begging him to remember that his great work was not yet done. There was a collective sigh of relief as the miracle of life began to re-enter his body.

Amina left before he opened his eyes. Bidding a silent goodbye she slipped out into the night, back to the obscurity of the desert. Years later she thought she spied him again in the East. She heard tales of a great teacher who walked the land reminding people that the nature of God is compassionate and loving. She did not try and connect with him. She knew her place in the scheme of things and that was enough.

Citrine

(protects against negative energy, increases psychic powers, soothes distress)

Liora looked up from her writing, surprised to see that the old monk was still there. He was sitting with a group of monks who were involved in an intense conversation and seemed not to pay him any attention. She noticed that he looked at her every now and then as if to ascertain that she too was still there. Thinking about their second encounter, she noted that the strange meeting was just as unexpected, and even more unsettling, than the first.

When she booked her most recent trip to Israel, Liora deliberately chose to stay in the center of Jerusalem, the city holy to Judaism, Christianity and Islam. Her hotel was right on the Via Dolorosa~ the route that Christ had walked carrying the burden of his cross on the way to his crucifixion, a street now in the heart of the Arab quarter.

From her hotel roof terrace she had a magnificent view over the Golden Dome of the Rock, the solemn stone wall of the

Temple Mount, and in the distance she could see the Mount of Olives. The sounds of the old city delighted her. The muezzin's Call to Prayer punctuated her days from the moment the first sliver of light broke the dawn, she could hear music from the Jewish quarter as it wafted over the rooftops, and the sound of the bells from the local churches beckoning the faithful.

But Liora found the Via Dolorosa itself a bit too chaotic. A cacophony of noise, the vibrant, bustling market-place that cuts through the center of the Arab quarter was crammed with little shops touting a riotous array of unorthodox goods ~ heaped mounds of pungent spices, bright plastic shoes, cheap bras, sticky sweet deserts, dubious copies of antiquities, and religious trinkets for every denomination. The hustle and bustle of Orthodox Jews, Arabs, priests, nuns, tourists, soldiers, all pushing their way along the small stone street, felt overwhelming to her as they formed the uneasy alliance that kept the city going.

One day she decided to follow Christ's path, stopping at all the Stations of the Cross and ending her walk in the Church of the Holy Sepulcher, that vast Romanesque building built by Emperor Constantine's mother Helena, in which can be found the last five Stations. To walk the Via Dolorosa, Liora discovered, is to experience first-hand the self-interest inherent in the drama of the Middle East. The way was not easy. People pushed and shoved along the narrow street ensuring that she swiftly reached the imposing church.

For centuries, she knew, pilgrims found the church vivid and compelling. And not much had changed. Monks were still swinging censers of pungent frankincense in long slow arcs as they prayed; hundreds of elaborate lamps continued to illuminate the gloomy interior throwing shadowy patterns on the intricately inlaid marble floors and across the monumental arches; somber clerics sternly supervised the visitors.

Liora could feel the fervent piety of worshipers as they wept at the stone where Christ was purportedly laid out, ducked into the tiny Greek Orthodox chapel to kneel at the spot where he was said to be buried, and waited patiently in the long slow line up the narrow marble stairs to touch for a brief moment a small fragment of the rock from Golgotha, or Calvary, the hill where the crucifixion took place.

Liora was particularly struck by the dissention amongst the various denominations that are the custodians of the church. Eastern Orthodox, Armenian Apostolic, Roman Catholic, Greek, Coptic, Ethiopian and Syriac Orthodox churches all have responsibilities within and around the building. She learned that the tension between these groups was surprisingly rife. For this reason, times and places of worship for each community is strictly regulated, but violence amongst them continues to break out every so often. How ironic, she thought, that due to the continuing dissention amongst the various Christian factions, the church is locked and unlocked daily by two neighboring Muslim families. And she was saddened at the way these followers of Christ's Way did not adhere to his loving message.

It was with some relief that after leaving the church, immense and awe inspiring as it was, she found herself in a little chapel belonging to the Russian Orthodox Alexander Hospice adjoining the great church on its back corner. Visitors, she noticed, walked right by it, few even thinking to stop in. Liora would probably never have gone inside either had she not noticed the old Greek Orthodox monk she had seen a few days earlier standing by the doorway.

Once again she felt his piercing glance, and then, indicating for her to follow him, he slipped purposefully through the simple doorway. His invitation felt more like an imperative and she wondered what he wanted to show her. Courage, she remembered reading somewhere, meant walking open-heartedly into life. And so taking a very deep breath, she followed.

Inside she found herself delighted by the Hospice's small chapel. Filled with golden icons and illuminated manuscripts, it was awash with natural light. As she entered, she noticed that the priest ignored the chapel and disappeared down an ancient stone staircase running beneath an excavated Roman Arch. Tentatively she followed him down the stairs, and turning a sharp left, found herself in a simple unadorned underground alcove.

The tiny space was sparse but in contrast to the busy-ness of the massive church, it was infused with great peace and stillness. The old monk seemed to have disappeared. In the center of the little room stood a large dark boulder, a simple but imposing iron cross bolted to its summit. The impact of the cross was like a bolt of lightning, direct and palpable. Suddenly Liora found herself utterly bereft, weeping for the very soul of the world, overwhelmed with thoughts about the nature of war and peace, pain and suffering, and the challenge of compassion.

It took her a while before she was ready to go out and face the world. Finally as she was leaving the building she passed a nun about to walk down the steps. "What is this place?" she asked. The nun looked surprised. "But of course this is the large rock from Golgotha, or Calvary, the site of the crucifixion," she replied. "How strange, usually it's only those who know who find themselves here."

Liora was suddenly left with the sensation that in this hushed and holy place, without even being consciously aware of it, something profound in her had been re-awakened. It was then that she remembered a lifetime in Medieval France when she too had been part of the clergy, and had herself, been very misguided....

ℰ𝒪

Kundun settled into his seat on the plane, happy to be next to the window. The couple sitting next to him nodded politely and ignored him for the remainder of the flight. He was glad for the space, because the gamut of emotions that had arisen with his memories during his taxi ride was exhausting. The taxi driver's questions had provoked much thought. He realized that although having the opportunity to explore both the Druze and Jewish religions was important to him, he had past karma with Christianity, and had in a number of his past lives had run-ins with representatives of the church. The first of those was in Medieval France, when he was a young woman and a local healer......

France: 13th C.

Anique heard the call of the morning dove all too soon. She was 24 and it was to be her last day. Strangely, she had been given the choice of how it was to end. She supposed she was blessed because having the choice at this late hour was a very unusual act to be bestowed by the tormentors of the Inquisition. She could only imagine there had been some kind of intervention, although at what level she was not sure.

Anique's crime was simple. She was a woman practicing the healing arts. And of course the irrefutable fact that she had given birth out of wedlock. It certainly made matters much worse that the baby was obviously the child of the priest, Pere Jean Baptiste, a senior member of the local archdiocese. The baby, a lovely little boy, she noted ruefully, had the same flaming red hair and beautiful brown eyes as his father, the man who stole both her innocence and ultimately her life.

Pere Baptiste came across her when he was out for a walk in the forest one evening. Tension had been building in him throughout the day as he studied in his monastic cell, and towards the evening he realized that he needed a brisk walk and fresh air in order to assuage the feeling. It was the 21st of October, the trees dropping their glorious red and gold leaves, the air already holding the chill of the coming winter. Bundling up against the cold, his rosary in hand, Pere Baptiste ventured out at great speed hoping to walk away his unrest. He walked briskly long past the hour of the setting sun, but the moon was up, the starry sky clear, and it was easy to see where he was going.

As he walked along the country path skirting the edge of some woods, Pere Baptiste suddenly caught the faint smell and sound of a bonfire in the wind. Like any great predator, he tracked and followed their trail and before long came upon a clearing amongst the thick grove of oak and plane trees. Stopping to listen, he heard it quite clearly ~ the unmistakable sound of women's voices rising and falling in a strange harmonic rhythmic chant, unfamiliar to Pere Baptiste. Of one thing he was sure ~ the chanting had nothing to do with the Mother Church.

Both curious and afraid, Pere Baptiste tiptoed as quietly as he could towards the scene, determined to avoid detection. And then he saw them. Heart pounding, he froze in his tracks. It was exactly as he had imagined~ a coven of witches immersed in some sort of demonic ritual. Of course, like everyone else, he had heard the rumors that there were witches about, but few had ever confirmed them. Now here he was, face-to-face with the damming evidence.

Although he could hardly control his anxiety and tension, he hid behind a copse of trees, determined to spy on the proceedings. Soon Pere Baptiste found himself absorbed in the intricacy and the intimacy of their ritual. He watched half-horrified, half-entranced as the women wove a complex circle invoking Arduina, patron goddess of the Ardennes. Their ceremony he overheard was a ritual for Samhain, the witches' sacred New Year, honoring the animal and ancestor spirits.

Aghast he watched them mark out the sign of the five pointed star, the pentagram, on the ground ~ 'Devil's work', he knew it to be. Deliberately, at each point of the star, their leader placed a beautiful stone, chanting as she did. Amber for earth, she intoned in a strong clear voice, reminding them about the importance of grounding and stabilizing. Aquamarine for water to calm the nerves and lift the spirits, Peridot for fire, a gift from the Sun to help reveal their inner sight and enhance their ability to look into the future, Smokey Quartz for the air element to develop the ability to receive messages from other realms, and Diamond for spirit, to aid them in attuning to the higher forces.

"Pagans," Pere Baptiste thought derisively as the women proceeded to invoke the four elements by placing a bowl of salt in the North of the circle to honor the Earth, a bowl of water in the West to honor Water, sweet smelling incense in the East to honor Air, and the bonfire in the South to honor the Fire element. Pere Baptiste was disgusted. He could not believe their utter ignorance, and was in dread as to which of those higher forces they were alluding as he could not imagine the highest force of all, His God, would ever condone such heretical practice.

And then the women began to dance, weaving themselves in beautiful complex circular patterns. To his chagrin and discomfort, Pere Baptiste found himself unable to move away. Most particularly, he found himself entranced by their leader ~ a graceful, lithe young woman, hypnotic in her movements, her long dark hair shining in the glow of the firelight. As he watched, Pere Baptiste felt himself becoming increasingly disturbed. He could feel the Devil's fire begin to play through him. Most particularly, he could feel the heat as it licked through his loins.

And then suddenly, it was over almost before he knew it. In retrospect Pere Baptiste only half-remembered the incident. He remembered that the dark beauty stopped suddenly mid-chant, and, staring into the darkness towards the copse of trees where he was hiding, the firelight flickering in her eyes, her clear strong voice called him out from his hiding place declaring for all to hear that he was in need of the herb Boneset to exorcise the confusion in his soul.

And he was aware that her gall, her dammed impertinence, enraged him. He would show her who was confused! In a flash he was upon her. He was vaguely aware that the others fled into the darkness and that she went limp beneath the power of his thrust. He was aware of her quiet sobbing as afterwards he stumbled away, unable to look at her wretchedness.

For a while after, there were hushed whispers that a member of the Inquisition had succumbed to the spell and enticement of a witch. He managed to maintain his anonymity until the baby was born. But when it arrived screaming its indignation with all the force and power of its origins and its flaming red hair, his identity could no longer be kept a secret. Hurriedly Pere Baptiste left the town before her trial commenced.

From afar he arranged for the baby to be sent to a convent. At least, he convinced himself, he could save that soul. And he also found it within his power to arrange that the woman be given the option to choose the manner of her death. Somehow this assuaged his conscience convincing him that he was dispensing an act of humanity in the gesture.

It haunted him for years to hear that she had chosen drowning over the fire. Pere Baptiste had a fear of water, but Anique knew the value of her choice. Like a good daughter of the moon, she chose the way of the feminine. She had attended many a birth, and was familiar with the flow of life. "The waters of life, they give and they receive" she thought as she faced the setting sun and slowly lowered herself into the river, quietly succumbing to the enfolding swirl of green, back to a watery womb.

Agate

(enhances creativity, strengthens intellect, harmonizes, protects, lessons envy)

Liora decided to stretch her legs and explore a little of the monastery guesthouse. It was an adjunct section of the church, built in the 1890s in the beautiful limestone that is the mandated material of all Jerusalem buildings. Like the rest of Jerusalem, it glowed golden in the light of the afternoon sun. Built in the style of a Gothic cathedral, Liora discovered its quiet simple rooms, peaceful retreats for pilgrims; a groin vaulted dining room; and most intriguingly, a small library its books tantalizing through locked glass doors. Aged leather chairs sat invitingly on beautiful oriental rugs. Liora loved the patterns and patina of old oriental rugs and knew a fair amount about them.

Searching for rugs from exotic parts of the globe had always been a joy for her, and for a while after her divorce she spent her time learning more about them. One store in particular enticed her because it was an Aladdin's cave filled with beautiful rugs and replete with heavy silver Afghani jewelry. One could get lost in the colors and patterns in the small jewel-like shop, and when the store owner suggested one day that she go down into his vast basement storeroom she was delighted. "Make sure you make it all the way to the back" he shouted, as she disappeared happily down the dark staircase.

Diligently she ambled along, slowly examining the mountains of rugs piled ceiling high, until she was way in the back, where to her astonishment she encountered a yurt ~ one of those wonderful round tented huts that shelter the nomads against the brutal winters on the Mongolian Steppes. Ducking through the simple carved wooden door, Liora sat quietly on the curved carpet-covered bench bathing in the dim light, enveloped in the quiet.

After the intensity of the store, the yurt was an oasis of calm and stillness. It's interesting, she noted, how stillness opens the way for inspiration, intuition and the unexpected. In this case it came to her in an odd form. Looking up at the lamp hanging from the center of the ceiling, she noticed how unusual it was. Brass, with six sides, it was inscribed with beautiful curving calligraphic verses from the Qur'an and crowned with a crescent moon and star. Something about it was so compelling that it suddenly seemed very important that she own it, and to know everything it represented.

Upstairs the owner took some convincing. "It's a very important lamp" he said slowly, "made by a very remarkable mystic." And, he concluded," It's not for sale". Somehow this only served to increase her ardor and after much coaxing, the owner eventually agreed to sell it to her, muttering enigmatically as he did, that she should really take care of it because "The mystic who made it did so with the energy of God himself, who is the Light of the Heavens and the Earth."

Synchronicity, Liora noted, plays wonderful games when one is being spiritually danced, so not surprisingly, in a local video store a couple of days later, Liora came across Peter Brooke's wonderful movie about a man searching for esoteric knowledge among Sufi groups with secret wisdom, "Meetings with Remarkable Men." The remarkable maker of her lamp would surely not have been surprised, she thought. Entranced by the movie, she became convinced that she was being drawn into the orbit of the Sufis.

Sufism, Liora soon to found out, was a spiritual path going back to the time of Abraham, considered to be not only the first Jew, but also the first Sufi due to his state of realization. For centuries Sufis traded and travelled the ancient silk routes, knowing full well that their journey was a far greater one than was outwardly visible.

Theirs is a journey towards the experience of Divine interplay between creation, manifestation, and the one who experiences it all ~ between the Lover, the Beloved and Love itself. This is the state that 13th century Sufi mystic poet Mevlana Jelal-ad Din Rumi had expressed as "I, you, he, she, we ~ in the garden of mystic lovers, these are not true distinctions." She learned that Rumi invited friends to enter into that mysterious 'paradise beyond all the false barriers' that we unconsciously create as an illusion of protection and survival.

Liora's heart was open and willing. And sure enough, not long after she bought the lamp she was invited into that mysterious garden and went gladly. The orchard she entered came in the form of the Sema Turn. The Turn is a moving meditation practiced by the whirling dervishes. It is imbued with symbolism, its spiritual goal to lose the separate sense of ego identity and merge with the fluid process of the dance of life itself.

Liora learned that the whirling Dervish dancers wear tall brown felt hats which symbolize the tombstone of the constricted ego; they wear black cloaks which they remove before they dance as a sign that they are removing that constricted ego consciousness; and their swirling white robes representing the purity of the soul. The steps of the dance, she learned, are simple and few. Stepping right foot around the left, right palm open to the sky receiving spirit, left palm turned downwards bestowing blessing on the earth. Spinning like the planets turning around the sun, her body turned around her heart.

Of course, Liora thought, whirling is an inherent pleasure. Children do it naturally. As a child she would whirl often. She remembered a trip to Mozambique taken with her family when she was young. They stopped at a beach north of the capital Maputo where the Indian Ocean was mill-pond calm. And out knee deep in water, a lone whirler was turning slow circles, joining sea to sky in the rhythm of some deep inner intuitive pattern. "We come spinning out of nothingness, scattering stars like dust," Rumi wrote.

Liora discovered that while turning, a person can experience absolute stillness. She felt as if she was perfectly centered, a threshold between the worlds of immanence and transcendence, the axis mundi centered in the heart, 'in the world, but not of this world.' In these moments, Sufis say, we become open vehicles for Divine 'Ishq', the love glue that holds the universe together. In those moments Liora felt herself drop her habitual sense of separation, as she opened to the dynamic interplay between action and stillness, vibrancy and silence, fullness and emptiness, the dance between doing and being. "The dervish is a doorway," Liora heard it said. "This is the way of the Dervish."

Liora's introduction to Sufism led, a few years later, to a trip to India. She had always been intrigued by the richness of the Indian culture and the Hindu religion, and she also wanted to explore the origins of the Sufi lineage she was most drawn to, the Chisti lineage. She loved the lineage's teaching about using the vibrations of music for healing and spiritual expansion, and most particularly, she was drawn to its teachings about the universal heart.

One morning she found herself sitting alone in the dhargah, or tomb, of Sufi Moineddin Chisti in Ajmer. The beauty of the dhargah, with its white stone, its fretwork screens, its elegant arches and columns, and rose petals spilling over the tomb and floor filled her with wonder. She was struck by how the outer beauty of the dhargah mirrored the beauty of the Murshid's message ~ by how the environment reflected an inner meaning and truth.

Suddenly she was awash with an incredibly powerful sense of déjà vu. She had been there once before as a schoolboy many centuries back.....

ꟷ

Kundun opened the travel magazine he found in the pocket of the seat in front of him. It was filled with beautiful pictures of an India he did not inhabit. There was a quiet natural rhythm to his life in the monastery. His days were filled with meditation, prayer, the joys of creating the Medicine Mandalas used for healing his community and the chores of monastery life. He lived in the mountains where the soaring peaks of the Himalayas reminded him daily of the soaring heights of his spiritual aspiration.

Looking now at the colorful pictures in the airplane magazine, he found himself absorbed in the beauty of the sandstone cities of Rajasthan. Kundun especially liked the pink color of the city of Jaipur, thoroughly enjoying the pictures of the antique jewels for which that city was famous. The pictures triggered in him a long forgotten memory ~ of a life in 16th century India. It was a life of teaching and devotion, and in particular, it was a life filled with the mission to right a great unspoken wrong from his lifetime in Medieval France…..

India: 1568

When word went out in the market place that they were looking for a teacher for the twelve year old son of a notable Brahmin family, Mohammad Latif Chisti knew immediately that the job should be his. He was not sure why, but somehow it felt very karmic to him. He was sure that it was he who needed to teach the boy. So on the day of the interviews, despite not being a Hindu, let alone a Brahmin, the confidence with which he walked into the room and the surety of his demeanor convinced the head of the household even before he offered his credentials.

He was not at all surprised to find that the boy, Sachdeva Khushwant Sharma, was difficult, carrying with him all the arrogance and entitlement of his youth, his class and his station. And yet he was pleased to find that he experienced sensitivity in the boy's parents. The father was refined and thoughtful if somewhat remote; the mother cultured, elegant and sensitive. He intuited that they would want their son to grow into the finest of human beings. And so it was that Muhammad Chisti came to develop a very unusual and ambitious educational program.

It took him a few weeks to formulate his plan. During this time he watched the boy from the shadows in an attempt to discover who he really was behind the mask of his immaturity and arrogance. It did not surprise him to find out that the boy was insecure and afraid of being bullied, but there was something in the boy's eyes that intrigued him ~ an unusual potential. It was clear to Mohammed Chisti that the boy needed to go out and meet the world in order to develop self-confidence.

And so he devised a plan. He would expose the boy to the great Moghul arts of the time, as well as to the sacred sites, and to the most important spiritual gurus in the country. It was a plan as ambitious as it was audacious, but it satisfied the social aspirations and culture of his parents and they readily agreed to it, realizing that their son would be occupied for some years and hopefully return fully prepared to take his place in society. As for the boy, he sulked for days when he heard his fate, but to no avail. He only reconciled himself to his circumstance when he realized his pleas fell on deaf ears, and he consoled himself with the fact at least his new teacher was very good at hitting a ball.

And so, sanctioned by the boy's parents, they set off on their unusual grand tour with an entourage of servants meant to bolster the journey, spy on the teacher and keep the boy safe. Mohammed Chisti soon tired of the large retinue and the inquisitiveness and restrictive lack of freedom that came with such a large party. As soon as they had enough months and miles between them, he jettisoned the entourage, paying them off for their co-operation and sending a message to the boy's parents mollifying them by explaining that too many people were holding them back, getting sick, and complaining, and that all this was taking away the focus of the boy's education. His wife, he explained, would be happy to do the cooking, the boy was well, and they would now be able to go to places where a handful of people would be much less of an intrusion than a whole caravan. In short, he wrote assuredly, the parents would save money and the boy would be better educated. Mohammed Chisti also made sure that the boy wrote to his parents just before they moved on, leaving no forwarding address but keeping communication open. And so began their great adventure.

Their first stop was the city of Ajmer in Rajasthan to visit the famed workshops of the Sultan. Mohammed Chisti had a relative who was one of the chief stone-cutters in the city and his influence opened many doors. The boy watched in awe as the craftsmen chiseled great slabs of shining white marble into columns, tabletops, boxes, and lotus-shaped water basins. Much to his surprise, the boy enjoyed the bustle of the workshops.

As if remembering some long forgotten dream, the boy started to come alive among the architectural elements. He was fascinated by the buildings he saw replete with jali, the lattice marble carved in beautiful patterns of minute geometrical and floral designs. He was amazed at how the craftsmen could call forth the spirit of nature in the chaotic midst of noisy stone-cutting and joshing conversations about daily life. It was here amidst marble channeled with lapis lazuli and malachite that the boy began to intuit the poetry in his soul. And it was here too that Mohammed Chisti was delighted to see that the boy became more accepting towards those he previously would have considered "beneath him".

After some time with the stonecutters, they moved onto the jewelry workshops in Jaipur, a city that served as an exclusive hub for jewelry making. Quieter places, the jewelry workshops were pools of focused endeavor as the craftsmen married gold with large precious and semi-precious gemstones and meenakari enameling, evoking birds, flowers and paisleys. The boy instantly recognized the gem-encrusted jewelry set with flat uncut diamonds, rubies and pearls on 24 carat gold using lac and fine pure gold foils. His mother had many such pieces, necklaces of varying lengths and thicknesses, nose-rings, bangles, tiny thumb-rings with installed mirrors, hip chains, waist belts, anklets and most particularly large bracelets of unique shapes all encrusted and embellished with gemstones. He was not sure why, but something about the stones both intrigued and disturbed him.

It was the first time on his trip, the boy realized, that he had consciously thought of his mother, and the thoughts caught him by surprise. As a young boy he had taken her for granted ~ she was always "just there". He had never engaged much with her, having a household full of servants to attend to him, and a beloved ayah to fulfill the role of nursemaid and nurturer. Now, confronted with this world of beautiful jewels, he began to consider his mother as a person ~ to wonder why she chose particular pieces for herself when tradesmen arrived with overflowing cases of jewels for her to choose from. He began to appreciate her refined taste and sensitivity to beauty, and in doing so he started to recognize her value. He confided these thoughts to his teacher, and Mohammed Chisti was gladdened at the softening of the boy's heart. If he accomplished nothing more, he thought, his job would have been done.

And yet, he accomplished much, much more. They journeyed through Rajasthan for many months, visiting the great palaces and forts, until Mohammed Chisti began to feel a need for a change of pace. He was craving the open space of the great desert that lay beyond the dusty edges of the towns they visited. Through a contact, he heard of the Rom people, nomads of the Kush desert, whose fierce independence and freedom of soul he wished to experience. He knew it would do the boy good.

And so their little group, for his wife had recently delivered twins, moved into the great silence. At first it frightened them and they huddled together around the night fires seeking solace even more than warmth. But gradually they became accustomed to the emptiness, even finding in it some ease and comfort, so that when after moving steadily North and Westward they encountered a lively group of Rom nomads, it was a bit of a shock.

Soon, however, they found themselves enveloped in the riotous joy of a people whose presence was as colorful as the dun sand was monotonous. Color exploded out of the Rom in the form of story, music and dance, and in their clothing ~ an exuberant clash of oranges, pinks and reds. But it was their music and dance that enticed them most. Evenings were spent around their bonfires filled with the intoxication of drums, flutes and stringed sarangi.

After a few weeks sitting spellbound at the edge of the group, Mohammed Chisti was delighted to see the boy put aside his natural reserve and join the other young men as they clapped and encouraged the women, feasting on the swirling dances of unveiling and undulating hips. And it was not surprising to him to find out that in the darkening aloneness as the fires died down, the boy discovered the wet joy of his developing manhood.

A few years had passed since they began their journey but Mohammed Chisti had two more important stops he wanted to make for the boy. He was delighted to see how naturally the boy embraced song, so when they left the Kush desert he took him to the city of Fatipursikri, to the tomb of his ancient relative, the great Sufi Suliman Chisti. It had been a long while since the boy insisted on the superiority of his Brahmin birth, and as he became more and more emotionally attached to Mohammed Chisti and his little family, although he never joined them on their carpets as they observed their call to prayer, he was now open to the beauty of their faith.

Fatipursikri enchanted the boy. He loved the teaching stories told by the local Sufis, and so enjoyed the trance rhythms of their Dhikr chants that he asked to learn the tabla in order to participate through drumming. He, who had felt so apart from life, was now starting to realize that all of life, as the Sufis taught him, was the music of God. And he found himself falling in love with life. He became infected with its richness and complexity, with the sheer exuberant joy of it. Mohammed

Chisti was pleased to note that as the boy learned to tune his musical instruments, he had begun to tune his soul.

Then Mohammed Chisti knew they were ready for their very last stop. It was time to introduce the boy to the tradition of his roots. Mohammed Chisti heard of a Swami in the ancient town of Varanasi, the oldest and holiest city in Hinduism situated on the edge of the Holy Ganges reputed to have been created by Lord Shiva himself. He had heard that the Swami was a fully enlightened being, and he too was eager to sit at the feet of such a master.

Swami Satchitananda lived on the banks of the Ganges not too far from the funeral ghats. He had deliberately chosen that particular spot in order to be close to the ashes, because they were reminders of the impermanence of all material things. At his stage of enlightened realization, he did not need the reminder, but he knew how powerful it was for his students.

The Swami was very discriminating about who he accepted as students. Mohammed Chisti's wife, for example, was not open to the teachings, and true to form, chose to spend her time with the women she met at the fruit and vegetable market. Initially when Mohammed Chisti and the boy approached the Swami he ignored them. However, as he continued to test them through his silence, and they continued to sit deferentially at his feet, he was pleased to note that their vibrations began to shift. The boy became quieter and Mohammed Chisti more and more still.

Hours were spent in the presence of the Swami in total silence. Mohammed Chisti was amazed at how, by simply sitting in the Swami's presence, questions that had plagued him for years simply melted away. The boy, for his part, began to notice little things he ordinarily would not have seen ~ insects crawling over the sand, the play of light as it reflected off the water, local vegetation. And then he shifted his focus to his inner landscape noting his thoughts and feelings, becoming aware that he was not holding on to them as much as he used to previously. Meanwhile, Mohammed Chisti expanded in his consciousness, met his inner silence, and his true Self.

Months passed in this way until one day the Swami indicated that he was going to be moving on. Five rich enlightening years had passed since they started their travels, and now it was time to return the boy to his family.

When they arrived back at his home, the boy's parents were overjoyed. The aloof impregnable personality who had left their house so very long ago, returned a true Brahmin ~ noble in his thoughts, warm in his heart, sincere in his soul, ready to engage the world and represent the family well. They were most pleased.

As for Mohammed Chisti, somewhere in the depths of his being, he knew he had helped to right a great karmic wrongdoing.

Tourmaline

(removes imbalances caused by conflict and confusion, harmonizes)

The monastery lunch Liora ordered consisted of simple vegetables and rice. She reflected on the time when she would have wanted more, a lot more, not only of food, but of everything. She wished now that she and her ex-husband had known better than to focus on the lavish and outward displays of their life. She wished too that they had honored the Native Americans on whose sacred land they had inadvertently built their house, and focused much more on a solid ground for their relationship.

One of the most authentically grounded people Liora came to know after her divorce was a dear Native American friend, Aypuka Peta Aypoecki – "One who walks in the dreams of others." He, like the old monk who was still sitting at a table at the periphery of her vision, walked this earth with the quiet certitude of one who knows his worth and his life's purpose. As the Faith Keeper and Medicine Man of his Nation, her friend's daily life demonstrated his deep understanding and connection to all.

She loved her friend's deep respect and profound compassion. She was in awe of how he committed to clean up local rivers, rehabilitate and return wolves to the wild, support delinquent adolescents by connecting them with elders in the community, and lead sweat-lodges for both the general population and prisoners on death row. She found his joy and creative exuberance contagious, admiring the fact that dancing, drumming, and playing the flute were just as important to him as those moments when, as a member of a group of Indigenous Elders from around the world, he brought healing to the planet.

As Liora thought of him, the worlds of the monks and the Native Americans seemed to merge, and from the deep recesses of her mind she glimpsed herself as a monk, ardent in purpose and conviction, on his way to rebuild a cathedral after its destruction by Native Americans during a war in the mid-seventeen hundreds……..

ꟸ

Before settling down to sleep, Kundun noticed that the person sitting in the seat next to him had taken out her rosary. Surreptitiously he watched her counting her beads, silently mouthing her payers. Kundun understood. He loved his wooden mala beads. They had worn smooth through years of daily use as he often intoned his mantras for hours at a time. He thought of his simple prayer wheel, its wooden handle also worn smooth as he twirled it around for hours, sending prayers out into the universe. And he considered how religious and spiritual practices differ and cause rifts between people even when the purported intent is the same. It always troubled him when people fought about their differing ideologies.

He thought back to a lifetime when he was confronted by the ardency of the Church's proselytizing, long ago in the 17th century when he was a Native American Faith Keeper and Medicine Man.....

New Mexico: 1694

It was almost dawn in the year AD 1694 and Friar Angelo was at prayers. He had been awake all night wrestling with an inner conflict. The truth was, he had arrived at the Mission in Santa Fe, New Mexico, convinced of his duty to spread the word of The Lord, Jesu Christo. He was determined to bring salvation to the heathens. Friar Angelo had never questioned his place in the church nor its mission. And yet here he was high up on a sandstone mesa 367 feet above the desert floor praying desperately for guidance and inner peace.

Friar Angelo had come, along with the newly appointed Governor Diego de Vargas whose duty it was to restore both civil and religious authority to New Mexico, to restore the churches destroyed during the Pueblo revolt of 1680. Friar Angelo arrived full of sincerity, convinced of his purpose and his place in a history, filled with the glory and the promise of salvation. And up until recently, of that he had no doubt.

One day soon after his arrival, Friar Angelo took a walk around the town's central Plaza. In his long brown monk's robe the heat was overwhelming and he hoped the stroll would afford him a chance to cool off a bit. He was also interested in getting a sense of the local Navaho people who he hoped to bring quickly to Christ.

Making his way around the busy market place Friar Angelo came across some of the local pottery and stopped intrigued. He was a lover of fine art and somewhat of a connoisseur, particularly of the beauty of religious art. This native pottery, he mused, lacked a certain refinement that was usually indicative to him of a high spiritual state.

Friar Angelo wandered around for a while, looking at and touching, many pottery pieces. Then quite unexpectedly, he happened upon.....well he could only call it a miracle! There amongst the myriad earthenware bowls, one tiny seed pot caught his eye. It was egg-shaped, a dark blue/black, highly polished, and decorated with deeply etched hummingbirds and flowers, little beads of turquoise set into the bird's eyes. The impact of the tiny pot shocked him.

Evocative and symbolic, the tiny piece seemed to him to embody far more than its visible contents. Holding it in his hands, Friar Angelo felt a perceptible change of vibration. He became aware of the red earth; the deep reverential love of this earth in the life of the potter; a glorious rightness of being embodied in material form. All his ideas of art slipped from his mind. The tiny pot was an exquisite manifestation of the Divine spirit.

Friar Angelo was aware that the potter had to be someone who lived with a deep connection to the essence and source of his being. He was rather surprised that here in the marketplace of heathens, one potter could open the way for spirit to flow through in a manner that was both inspired and creative. And he was amazed at how it opened the way for him to experience that glorious mystery.

Although disconcerted to be feeling such depth from an object made by a heathen, Friar Angelo recognized immediately that such an accomplished artist would be perfect to help him with the art in the chapel. Upon discreet inquiry he soon found out that the potter was the local Hatalii, or Medicine Man, who lived in a nearby pueblo. A man named Niyol, 'The one who talks with the Wind'. Friar Angelo was curious about such a person, and could only imagine the heights to which the potter might rise by accepting The Lord into his heart. He was determined to meet him.

The meeting took place one Friday after morning chapel. For some inexplicable reason prior to the meeting Friar Angelo was restless, pacing around his little room. He could not understand why he was feeling so nervous about the meeting, but his intuition told him it would be an encounter of some significance.

Friar Angelo was moved when he met the Medicine Man who was older than he expected, but still strong in his body, his skin bronzed with the kiss of the sun, his hair still dark and long. Friar Anglo found him simple, yet powerful in his presence. He invited him into the chapel with the sole intention of impressing him with the beauty of the space and the power of its religious artifacts.

Niyol walked slowly around the chapel noting everything, listening politely as Friar Angelo talked far too quickly and far too ardently. The Friar was sweating, well aware that his discomfort had nothing to do with the heat. Niyol's quiet steady gaze was disquieting, as if he could see right into the very depths of his soul. Flustered, Friar Angelo ended the meeting early and quite suddenly.

It was some time before he met with Niyol again. He found himself thinking about him frequently, convincing himself that the conversion of such a man would afford him great merit in heaven, not to mention the admiration of the church fathers. Finally Friar Angelo gathered up the courage to call for another meeting. This time Niyol invited him to his home in the pueblo.

It was late afternoon when Friar Angelo arrived at the simple adobe hut on the edge of the pueblo central square. There he found Niyol sitting in the fading sunshine on a simple wooden bench playing a flute. Friar Angelo could tell that the flute was made with as much care as the little pot that had affected him so profoundly. He noted that the wood was beautifully smooth, and he was impressed by a carved turquoise stone in the shape of a hawk attached to the flute by a simple piece of leather. But more than the physical beauty of the instrument, it was the music that moved him. Haunting in its loveliness, Friar Angelo soon found himself swept into a longing that was as deep and as ancient as his very soul.

After a while, as the sun's red glow stained the horizon, Niyol's wife brought them a plate of wild potatoes cooked with herbs and pinion seeds. A quiet woman, she sat politely a little way off on the side listening as Niyol explained the rhythm of his daily life. Friar Angelo soon found out that Niyol's life was filled with ceremony and the magic of shamanism. Softly Niyol explained that his family had always held the role of Medicine Men and Faith Keepers, and as such were messengers for the spirit world, and healers for their community.

Niyol paused and regarded Friar Angelo carefully, not wanting to take the man too far out of his comfort zone. But when he continued his voice was strong in its conviction. "We are strong and powerful in our belief," he said. "nurturing and healing our relationships with one another, our families and our communities." Friar Angelo nodded. That he could understand.

But it was what Niyol said next that most confounded and intrigued him. "The thing is," Niyol emphasized, "we are not apart from the earth, we are of the earth. We are this place. As an indigenous person I feel the trees, I feel the plants, I feel the animals and I feel the wind. And this affords me a deep compassion for all of life."

The conversation left Friar Angelo disturbed. It was not so much that the ideas were perplexing, although he found them very unusual, but rather, he reflected, as he walked slowly home, that he had not expected them here in the wilds of the Americas. In fact, the only people he could possibly have attributed them to, until now, were the founder of his Order, St. Francisco of Assisi; and of course The Lord Jesu Christo himself. That did not sit well with him. And yet, he could not help but admit, there was no arrogance nor artifice about the man Niyol. Friar Angelo found him unassuming and humble in a way that only a man who speaks his truth and truly knows himself can be.

Friar Angelo began to spend more and more time with the Medicine Man. He wanted to learn about the Navaho ways. The Diné nation, he learned soon enough, was what the people called themselves. He learned that their life was particularly rich in ceremony and ritual. He learned about their sand altars that depict the characters and incidents of myths, and how to build sacred homes. He learned about the ceremonies for the planting of crops, and about the songs and prayers that accompanied all they held sacred.

But Friar Angelo was especially interested to hear about the sacred ceremonies. Niyol taught him about the Blessing-way that honors the divine feminine as nurturer, and Friar Angelo stretched his imagination trying to relate it to the compassionate influence of Mother Mary. It was easier for him to relate to the ceremony of the Protection-way that honors the divine masculine as a protector-provider because, he realized, honoring God-the-father was the substratum of his personal faith.

The Diné's great nine-day purification and cleansing ceremony for the restoration of beauty, harmony, balance and health in the world also made sense to him, and he could find coherence in it with the purification of the baptismal right. And although he found the Dine community greatly in want of saving in the name and body of Christ, he could understand that they were trying to contact the Holy Ghost when they practiced their journeys to the spirit world.

The more he learned of the Diné's spirituality, the more imperative it became to him that he teach Niyol about the Christian path to heaven and Eternal Life. And Friar Angelo began to share with Niyol the beauty of his own faith, hoping to draw him and his people into his flock.

He recounted the story of the life of Jesu, his death and miraculous resurrection. He explained about His Lord's great healing miracles, and the profundity of the parables. He talked earnestly about the liturgy and about his favorite ritual, the Rosary of the seven joys, explaining how he would weave a crown of prayers for the Holy Mother with rounds composed of recitations of "Our Father" and "Hail Mary". And because they both loved song, he taught Niyol his favorite Gregorian chants that they sang together long into the dark nights. Somehow, during the sacredness of that practice, they found themselves crossing the divide into a friendship woven of faith and true communion.

One day Niyol asked Friar Angelo to join him in the sacred Medicine Wheel ceremony. Niyol explained that the purpose of the Medicine Wheel was to honor the four directions; the four elements of earth, water, fire and air; and was a profound pathway to truth, peace and harmony. The ceremony left Friar Angelo feeling rather uneasy. He associated the ritual with Paganism, and he had strong issue with Paganism. Friar Angelo began to feel concerned that instead of leading Niyol to the One true God, he might be at risk of being led astray himself.

And to make matters worse, word amongst the Church Fathers was that he was being seduced by the Devil. His actions were called severely to task and he was threatened with excommunication. The situation had come to a head. Friar Angelo was ordered to search his conscience.

And so it was that he found himself high up on the mesa in the pre-dawn hours in an effort to pray and meditate. The irony of the practice did not escape him. He knew that Niyol would often go out to the top of the desert mesa on a vision quest in order to communicate with Great Spirit.

As the first golden light tinted the great open sky, his answer came to him. He needed to sever his relationship with Niyol. It was time to go ~ to return to the solitude of his calling. He would request a transfer, to St Catherine's, the Orthodox

Monastery of the God-Trodden at the top of Mount Sinai in the Holy Land.

Ruby

(children, protection,
devotion, fosters relationship)

Like many Middle Eastern courtyards, the monastery garden was arranged around a central fountain. Its blue, white and black tiles reminded Liora of the decorative tile work she enjoyed on a recent trip to Morocco, where she had gone because she was drawn to the International Music festival in Fez.

Liora loved Fez. She loved the beautifully renovated riaad where she stayed in the old city. The old house with its secret inner courtyard appealed to her sense of fantasy with its winding staircases and hidden rooms. She also loved the cornucopia of zellij tiles in myriad tessellated patterns on buildings all over the town, and the carved wooden doors and windows she found on the architecture all over the city. She could easily understand why Fez was nominated as a World Heritage Site.

She spent enjoyable days visiting potteries, the Jewish cemetery on the outskirts of the Mellah, and trips into the High Atlas Mountains. She hiked into the interior to explore waterfalls and slow meandering streams, passing by tiny Berber villages mysteriously shut off from the world by high mud walls, and enjoyed the fishing villages strewn like jewels along the coast.

But it was in the winding alleyways of the old Medina in the city of Marrakech that she felt particularly at home.......

ꝏ

Thoughts of his coming visit with the Druze Sheik flitted through Kundun's mind. What most impressed him about the man was his dedication to peace. The Druze, he found out, were scattered across northern Israel, Lebanon and Syria and were fiercely loyal to the land where they lived. With the tensions in the area, they often found themselves on opposite sides of political and geographical divides. As a consequence, in an attempt to ameliorate the painful situation battling families against families, they became peacemakers.

Because Tibetan Buddhism teaches that everything is interconnected, Kundun recognized that he would find a deep sense of himself reflected in both the pain and the beauty of the Holy Land. He was interested to see how people lived in that part of the world with its continued tensions reflecting the blood and hopes of history. He admired the Sheik for reaching across the ancient divide to find friendship, not only with his fellow Druze, but with others of all the different faiths of that ancient land.

Holiness, Kundun understood, came in the meeting of the so-called "other", and of recognizing it in one's own face. This understanding lived deep in his unconscious, fortified centuries before in another country on the Mediterranean, not very far from the Middle East.....

Morocco: 1860

Aliyah was late. Sarah was waiting patiently, guessing the reason was as usual, the busy traffic. But, she acknowledged to herself, they were both used to waiting. Patience was the rule of their profession, and they both knew how to deal with it.

Aliyah sat in her horse-drawn carriage observing the constant flow of the traffic. Going anywhere in Marrakech, she thought, is an altogether spiritual affair. If one was serious about getting from start to finish in one healthy piece, one had to invoke the higher gods and make a heart-felt pact with them. Road rules in Marrakech were completely ignored and streets marked with two lanes usually carried six in a complex weaving mass of carriages, donkey carts, pedestrians, horses, camels, and feral cats. As a passenger, she surrendered any semblance of control, allowing the driver of her carriage to glide into the nearest gap whenever he could.

Aliyah thought about the first time she met Sarah so long ago while they were both out in the countryside buying herbs. It was as normal a meeting as it was strange. Normal, she thought, because they had struck up an easy conversation ~ and strange because it was so unusual for members of such different parts of the Marrakech community to come into contact with each other at all. Interestingly, it turned out that they had a lot in common.

The herb garden was hidden down a dusty, badly rutted road in the tiny village of Tensift-Al-Haouz in the fertile Ourike Valley. The gardens sold medicinal herbs needed for their work, and time spent there was an aromatic treat. Aliya and Sarah arrived at the same time. After greeting the women who sat near the gate gossiping whilst shelling argan nuts to be used for teas and massage oils, they made their way slowly along the little stone paths that separated the herb gardens, pointing out their desired purchases. The day was beautiful, the air sweet and redolent with the scents of mint, sage, rosemary and lavender.

After completing their purchases, as was the custom, Aliyah and Sarah ended their shopping in a black Berber tent, comfortably settled on brightly colored cushions, in happy anticipation of refreshment. Glancing at each other shyly they felt an immediate kinship. They soon discovered that they were both qabla, midwives, who used herbal infusions of mint, thyme, cinnamon and cloves to ease the pain of their client's contractions. By the time their tea arrived, in tiny bisque cups filled with a delicious combination of sage, rosemary, thyme, argan, water and honey, and augmented with fresh mint leaves, they felt like they had known each other forever.

Because the tea was a detoxifier, their conversation turned naturally to the topic of release and purification. It was a few weeks before Rosh Hashana, the Jewish New Year, and Sarah explained that as a Sephardic Jewess, in spiritual alliance with the New Year, she would perform a ritual for purification called Taschlikh, or 'casting off'. The word, she explained, derived from the biblical passage (Micah 7:18-20) and recited at the ceremony: "You will cast all your sins into the depths of the sea."

That year, Sarah told Aliyah, she intended to visit relatives in Essaouira, the beautiful white seaside town partially sheltered by the island of Mogador. There, on the dock of the ancient harbor, she would throw breadcrumbs into the waters, symbolically casting off what she no longer wished to carry in her life, metaphorically washing herself clean. Sarah explained that the process of releasing is understood to work on many levels, the physical, the emotional and the spiritual, thereby relieving the soul of its burdens and opening the way for the fresh and the new. Aliyah was entranced. Her people were Sufis, mystics who recognized Divinity everywhere, and she was receptive to learning about other religious paths.

Soon after their first meeting, upon hearing that Aliyah was a lover of architecture and of sacred spaces in particular, Sarah invited her to visit an old synagogue in the Mellah, the ancient Jewish Quarter of Marrakech. One fine afternoon, they met in the courtyard of the synagogue with its beautiful star-shaped fountain. They passed the small windowless room where the caretaker sat crouched on the earthen floor, peeling vegetables just as her ancestors had done for centuries. The interior of the synagogue had not changed much either ~ softly yellowing painted walls, wooden benches worn smooth by centuries of pious backsides, blue and white zellij wall tiles. Behind purple velvet curtains, the ark held a single Torah from the 1700s wrapped carefully in an embroidered turquoise cloth.

After visiting the women's gallery upstairs, Sarah took Aliyah down the steep stairs to the mikvah, the ritual bath cut deep into the earth, hidden from view below the synagogue floor. Here in the still, dark, archaic pool of rainwater, women through the ages bathed before their marriages, cleansed and blessed their new dishes, prepared themselves for the Sabbath, and marked their readiness to procreate after the time of their menstrual blood. Aliyah was fascinated. She determined to invite Sarah to visit the place she enjoyed for her own personal purification rituals.

A stark contrast to the ritual mikvah, 'The Secret of Marrakech' was beautiful, its décor simple and sensuous. The midnight blue, almost black, walls were painted in the beautiful technique called tadelakt, the traditional coating used for hammams and bathrooms, and were an apt metaphor for the purification process. Tadelakt, Aliya explained, was a Berber word meaning "to rub", ~ the paint consisting of waterproof lime plaster polished over and over with olive soap and a river rock until it acquired a silky luxurious glow ~ like the soul, they agreed, worked over by life itself.

A dark limestone passageway and softly lit lanterns led the way to the inner sanctum ~ a beautiful dark secret of a room with heated limestone benches and a pool of floating rose petals. Surrendering themselves, in the age-old woman's ritual, to the attendant's practiced hands, they were scrubbed clean with an intoxicating mixture of argan oil, honey and the ground pits of black olives. Then they were washed down with the water from the rose pool and massaged with an almond-infused argan crème.

In the intimate closeness of that hushed environment, they found themselves talking about the more difficult aspects of their work. They had both been present for wonderful live births, but the nature of their work meant that they were also present to tend families grieving the loss of a dream ~ of babies who were not born to live, or who passed on very quickly. It was sensitive work, and very tender. They both felt the weight of it and perceived in it the profound initiation into the Sacred Feminine. The Shekinah, the Divine Spirit as it manifests in the world, is what Sarah called it.

And so their unusual friendship continued as an ongoing pleasure and support for many years. Often they alternated trips to the gardens with trips to the hammam. And once Sarah braved the wrath of her God and joined Aliya in the outer courtyard of the mosque and its attached madrassa school because her friend really wanted her to see the beauty of its design. Sarah was entranced with the exquisite mosaic work of the building, its layered and boundless geometric patterns of inlaid precious stones depicting life under the stars, the infinitude of the desert, the lush visions of vines and paradise in the sinuous calligraphy of Qur'anic verses.

And so it was that after many years of friendship, Aliyah's carriage finally arrived at the herb garden where they had first met. She found her friend already relaxed, cup of tea in hand quiet in her strength and grace. Aliyah was reminded of the presence of her Murshid, her spiritual teacher. She remembered telling Sarah once what a great artist he was. Sarah was intrigued and wanted to know what kind of art he did and was delighted when Aliyah answered "Ahh, Sarah, you should see the way he pours a cup of tea!"

Now there she was, her wonderful friend, mirror of her heart, immersed in her reverie, picture-perfect in the beautiful garden, enveloped in a cloud of exotic white, red and black butterflies. In the distance, the High Atlas Mountains shimmered in the summer heat.

Not long afterwards Sarah left this world. Aliyah attended her funeral standing respectfully to the side, aware that their friendship would not be understood by most of Sarah's friends and family. The service touched her deeply, especially the Yizkor prayer for the dead. 'Remember', the words said, and she did ~ the bond between them forever held in her heart.

Moonstone

(Rhythms, cycles, destiny, lunar, emotional, intuitive)

Liora was surprised that the old monk was still there, and she started feeling uncomfortably that perhaps she was the only one who could see him. Others passed in and out of the courtyard and walked right past him without so much as a nod of acknowledgement. She shivered. A sudden breeze brought with it the memory of her death in her second-to-last lifetime.

It was after her first visit to England when she was 17 that she began her past life regression sessions. She had such a strong sense of deja-vu and an innate knowledge of the English countryside that she was determined to find out whether she had ever lived in England in another life.

On the day of her first session, she arrived at the appointment feeling a mixture of curiosity and skepticism, but was not really surprised when, during the regression she met herself as a young English girl in search of something very important...

ꝏ

Kundun adjusted his maroon zhen wrapping it neatly over his shoulder. He enjoyed the simple freedom of his monk's robe, and was happy that the simplicity of his dress exemplified his focus on renunciation. There was a sweet humility in his life as a monk consistent with the truth of his state of realization.

He knew he had lived as a monk before, as a Swami, teaching the wisdom of the Vedas, the Hindu sacred texts; the consequences of karma; and the importance of the dharma. He also knew that he had travelled to teach the wisdom of Hinduism in the early 20th C when many people in England and Europe where becoming fascinated with the spiritual teachings of the East…..

England: 1905

On the morning of her tenth birthday Gwyneth awoke with a great sense of urgency. As the sun arose pale through the tall trees, spreading its thin rays across the expansive green lawn, she slid down the side of her four-poster rosewood bed onto the Oriental rug, and ran across the room, pulling urgently on the mirrored wardrobe. Slipping quickly out of her nightdress, she put on her prettiest white muslin frock, the one with a great big sky-blue bow.

It was a good thing that Mummy was sleeping late that morning, she thought. Her mother would definitely not approve of Gwyneth going out on a frosty early morning in her best new dress. But Gwyneth was on a mission she felt was really important. She was going hunting for treasure.

Tiptoeing silently through the house, she quietly slid open the long brass latch of a French door leading from the morning sitting room onto the flagstone terrace, raced down the curved stone steps, across the beautifully manicured lawn, and slipped into the dank woods bordering the large garden.

It was quiet at that early hour, the dew still wet on the grass, and Gwyneth could sense the presence of magic. She would not have been surprised to stumble across a group of fairies playing amongst the fallen logs, or hiding behind the stalks of the yellow cowslips and delicately scented primroses carpeting the ground. Her very own magic carpet, she thought, delighted.

Gwyneth loved the woods. They were often her refuge after tedious lessons, and it was amongst the tall trees that she hid after being reprimanded. The woods were extensive, and only on the rare occasion would she come across anyone at all. Occasionally she would meet the game keeper setting rabbit traps, but usually it was her private kingdom. She loved how she felt amongst the flora and fauna. If pressed she would have said that the plants, animals and insects were her real friends.

This particular early morning she was blissfully alone. As she hurried along, a nest, high up in the branches of a sturdy oak tree caught her eye. She was up in the tree in a flash. Peeking into the nest, she spied five tiny speckled blue eggs ~ robin's eggs. This, she sighed with pleasure, was exactly the treasure she was searching for!

Gwyneth was drawn to round shapes. Her parents were landed gentry, cultured, curious, the heart of a fashionable set fascinated with Spiritualism, Theosophy, and everything Oriental. They lived in a large cream-colored stone house in

Surrey and held many large gatherings populated by the most interesting people.

Recently, when she should have been in bed, but was eavesdropping at the top of the stairs, she overheard her parents talking about the significance of circles. Their study of sacred geometry taught that circles and ovals were most important shapes because they denoted wholeness and the movement of the planets. Gwyneth did not exactly understand it all, but she was convinced the egg's shape contributed to its worth.

She knew the egg was life-giving and had a brief moment of regret as she secreted a perfect egg out of the nest, justifying her action as somehow connecting to a great universal mystery based on what she had overheard about its shape. Back in her house, in her bedroom, Gwyneth added the egg to her other treasures, wrapping it carefully in a monogrammed lace-edged handkerchief, and hiding it in her special carved ivory jewelry box.

Not long after that she was confined to bed. On the morning of the treasure hunt she had caught a chill that became a raging fever. Her last days were spent contemplating her treasures :~ a large engraved golden bead, three small seed pearls, a pressed butterfly, her blue robin's egg, and most especially a string of sandalwood mala beads given to her by a stranger visiting her parents one Saturday afternoon a few months prior to her illness. She loved to think about the stranger.

When she met him a few months before, he made a huge impression on her. He was tall, dark and in her eyes, most handsome in his long saffron robes. Gwyneth was sure he was a prince. Her parents called him 'Swamiji', and she could tell he was someone very important by the way they listened to his every word. She noticed that the other visitors, who came that afternoon specifically to meet him, also seemed to think he was someone very important.

But Gwyneth felt like she had a special connection to him. What struck her most about him was the way he looked at her. He seemed to want to make sure she was a part of the afternoon proceedings, and that made her feel very important. The stranger had unsettling eyes, warm and disquieting. Looking into them felt very odd, yet Gwyneth did not want to look way. She felt a certain dispassionate reserve from him, and yet, oddly, at the same time she felt as if she was falling into the loving center of the universe. Gwyneth was thrilled when, towards the end of the afternoon, he took the beautiful mala beads from his neck and gave them to her.

But even more important to her was that he bent down to her level, and whispered to her in a hushed voice that he had a very special secret message for her. "Always remember who you are my dear," he said in his strange accent. "You are made of love. This means that you can be nothing but loving, and nothing but loved." For a little girl whose parents were very busy and who was often alone, the words held more significance for her than anyone could imagine. In that moment Gwyneth felt a great peace wash through her. It was impossible for her to talk about it and she never did. The message became her very special secret and her most precious treasure.

Not long after her foray into the woods, Gwyneth left this world. Hovering above the scene of her funeral, she saw that she was buried in her best white dress, the blue satin lining of the mahogany coffin matching her sky-blue bow. Her treasure chest was placed beside her, and she wished she could tell her weeping parents that she had taken the real treasure with her, her special secret treasure, the knowledge of her inherent nature whispered to her by her prince.

And then she let go, swirling into the cosmic soup of the astral plane, rich with the archetypes of art, mathematics, dreams, archetypal memories, and myriad stories. The record of her English life forever stored in the archives of the Akashic records; the record of her secret treasure forever stored in her heart.

Prehnite

(connects the will and the heart, attunes to the highest good)

The afternoon sun was beginning to cast long shadows across the courtyard garden, lending it an air of mystery. It had been a long day of self-reflection, the emotions of deeply held memories and impressions intense as they came to light. Liora was tired and needed to walk a little. She noticed that the old monk was no longer in the courtyard.

Having no desire to go back to her hotel, Liora made her circuitous way to the Jewish quarter. She arrived at the Western Wall of the Temple Mount just as the sun was setting. Like most evenings the square in front of the wall was full of people praying. The men's side of the dividing fence was a sea of prayer shawls and murmuring voices. The women, more sedate in their manner, made their way quietly to the wall, slipping fervent prayers into the cracks between the large stones that had stood as testimony to their faith for more than 2,000 years.

Rubbing her hands across the golden stones, Liora begged softly for forgiveness, guidance and clarity. "Avinu Malkeinu", she prayed, "Our Father, our King, please forgive my trespasses, throughout my lifetimes whether they were by omission or commission." It was an address to God from the depths of her soul, the solemnity of which was usually associated with Yom Kippur, the Day of Atonement, and reserved for situations of extreme human need. The woman next to her looked up in surprise. Liora smiled uncomfortably. Then she noticed the numbers tattooed on the woman's arm, and was immediately plunged into images from her last life ~ a life as an extremely courageous young woman in Nazi Germany.......

ࢨ

Israel, Kundun discovered, is a land of contrasts, at once ancient and very modern, and the architecture of Ben Gurion airport is a testimony to that. Kundun was impressed with the way the architect had played with those contrasts, juxtaposing glass walls with intricate Byzantine mosaics. He had not expected it. But then he was to find out that there would much on this trip he would not have expected.

Of course he was well aware of the immense history he would meet in the ancient land, and was both fascinated by the country's diverse culture, and saddened by its painful political schisms. He knew the Dalai Lama had recently met with some Rabbis in order to try and understand how Judaism had survived in the diaspora for two thousand years, and during that meeting, discovered that there were also profound similarities between mystical Judaism and Tibetan Buddhism.

Kundun mulled over those similarities as he waited for his bags. Both traditions, he understood, recognize that overcoming the ego is the main prerequisite to spiritual awakening, and both honored the interconnectedness and underlying unity of life. He was surprised to learn that mystical Judaism, like Buddhism, had a belief in rebirth, what the Jews called gilgul, loosely translated as 'recycling' and that they both emphasized cosmic justice, karma as it was known to him. Waiting patiently for his bag, he smiled, knowing they both also valued equanimity through life's travails, both great and small.

But most gladdening to Kundun's heart was that they both cultivated respect for all creatures and for compassion-in-action. For him the importance of this "Tikkun Olam" as Judaism called it, was the basis of his Bodhisattvic vow to participate actively in the restoration to wholeness of the World Soul. Kundun reflected on how he might have done just that in his previous life during the 2nd World War....

Swiss/French/German Borderlands: 1941

This time when the call came it was early afternoon. Jean-Luc was always on alert expecting the call, but he never knew when it would come, nor could he ever predict its particular nature. Sometimes it came in the form of a note dropped in his shopping basket, or slipped into a pocket of his jacket; sometimes as a word mumbled by a passing stranger.

As a single young man, a farmer who loved skiing and the occasional jaunt into town to meet women, living in the countryside in the shadows of the Alps made it somewhat easy for him to disappear for a few days without arousing too much suspicion. Unlike other members of the Resistance who had to make complex and elaborate reasons to travel, the leeway his life-style afforded him proved fortuitous. He knew that was partly the reason he was recruited. And of course, as a skier who regularly skied off-piste, he was fearless and knew the mountain passes well.

The voice on the other end of the phone was unfamiliar to him ~ a woman this time. She chatted merrily about this and that as if she had known him forever. Jean-Luc was always en-garde for a word slipped in the wrong way in the wrong moment, his intuition on hyper-alert. Did she call him "Mon cher" one time too many? Was the code stressed with too much emphasis? Just recently a good friend had disappeared. One could never be too attentive. Members of the Resistance had become all too aware of their fate should they be caught.

Hurriedly, Jean-Luc gathered together his belongings preparing for his trip. Everything had to be consistent with his story; nothing should invoke the slightest suspicion. He packed a suit in his backpack ~ something he would have only worn under duress, or if he had to go to mass on Christmas Eve. But this meeting, he was informed, was to take place in a big town some miles across the border in Germany, and dressing up for dinner was expected.

It took Jean-Luc a few days of intense hiking, making his way along barely perceptible game paths in the shadows of moonless nights, evading mountain villages and the possibility of alerting dogs. In truth he was a loner. He loved the mountains and really enjoyed backcountry hiking and skiing.

Ever since he was a boy he had spent time exploring these mountains, hunting with his father, learning how and where to avoid detection.

Just before he reached Germany, Jean-Luc changed into his suit, hid his pack beneath some rocks, and slipped soundlessly over the border. It was a Saturday, and it was not unusual to meet a local farm boy hitching a ride into town. With his blonde hair, blue eyes, and sense of familiarity, he aroused no suspicion. His age too was in his favor. Many a young man was known to slip across the border for a clandestine meeting with a dubious lady and turning a blind eye or a knowing wink was common amongst the locals.

The assignation was to be in a very public restaurant. Jean-Luc was somewhat surprised, and nervous. This was not the usual protocol. Typically he was left a note in some obscure place or passed his orders bumping into someone in the park. This time, however, his orders were to meet his "date" for dinner in a beautiful restaurant connected to the medieval plaster and timber inn on the town square next to the church. Not at all what Jean-Luc would deem clandestine.

He arrived a little early, wanting to scope out the situation, and found that a table was booked in his name at the back of the room. Jean-Luc was glad of its position because it gave him a full view of the place. The dining room was typical of finer restaurants in that area ~ starched white linen tablecloths, silver cutlery, crystal wine glasses. He now understood the request for a suit. Obviously this dinner was meant to signal "an occasion" to anyone vaguely interested.

The restaurant was full of diners, many of whom were noisy German soldiers drinking a lot, making the most of their evening off. Jean-Luc glanced around casually trying to ascertain whether there was any sign of danger. His papers were in order and his alibi tight, but it was difficult to still his nerves. He was glad for his ability to blend in.

The same however, could not be said for the strikingly beautiful woman who came in soon after and made her way directly to his table. Her beauty caused a sensation and she was dressed to provoke attention. Had she not been holding a black pocket book with a red butterfly clasp, he would never have supposed she was there to meet him. For a moment, as the German soldiers tried to catch her eye, he thought he might have been set up. She ignored them however, with the panache of one who truly knows her value.

After a warm kiss on both cheeks, she slipped into her chair, her hand lingering lovingly on Jean-Luc's arm. He was struck by how naturally she flirted with him, finding himself responding easily, contrary to his shy nature. He soon noticed that their easy conversation about nothing in particular made them of less interest to the other diners, and he began to marvel at how they were hiding 'in plain view'. He was quite impressed at the mastery of her deception, although he was a little baffled at no mention of his assignment.

It was only after their meal, when they left the restaurant, her arm securely tucked in his, that she was able to steer him around the square, behind the church to a waiting car. Once inside she indicated that they were not to speak, but snuggled up to him and deftly slipped a wedding ring on his finger. He noted that she put one on too. At the edge of town, they swopped to another car, this one a small grey French Deux-Chevaux that would also draw little attention. It was only once they were alone inside, and he had driven in the direction she indicated that she told him the nature of their mission.

They were to travel as a newly married couple for the first hour and a half, and then as a young family after they picked up two little Jewish children who they were to deliver to a convent near Langres in the French region of Alsace. The convent had agreed to hide the children from the Gestapo for as long as was necessary. Their assignment was to take back roads through the farmlands, and cross into France without causing any suspicion. The woman told him that she heard that knowledge of the area was his forte, and that was why she agreed to go with him on the mission. Jean-Luc felt the weight of her expectations compound the responsibility already heavy on his shoulders. He was surprised at how much he wanted to please her.

It surprised him too that after her chatty flirtatiousness at dinner, she now chose to continue the journey in silence. Jean-Luc masked his disappointment with the rationale that the less they knew of each other the better. Should they be caught they would genuinely not be able to divulge important and compromising information. They drove slowly and quietly, lights off, their only communications the hand signals she used to indicate the direction he was to take.

Around 2.30am they turned onto a small dirt road that led through a field of sunflowers, their petals closed and forlorn looking at this time of the night. At the end of the dirt road they turned into the yard of a remote farm where the woman directed him to an old timber barn. She remained in the car when he went inside.

Inside, the barn was pitch dark, the only light pale slivers that passed through the narrow slats of the ancient wooden roof. A strong smell of hay permeated the air. Jean-Luc sat down on a small bale and waited. The only sound of which he was aware was the intense beating of his heart. It was a full 20 minutes before he realized he was being watched. Then furtively, without seeing who handed them to him, Jean-Luc became the guardian of two reed baskets each containing a small sleeping child.

They left the farm as they had come, incognito and in silence. Jean-Luc was unaware of the faces or the names of their contacts. He drove slowly towards the border, crossing at dawn, the woman nursing one of the babies with a bottle of milk she found in its basket. Jean-Luc convinced the bleary-eyed border guards in his impeccable accent of a family emergency that compelled him to take his little family on such a trip at such an ungodly hour. He was relieved that the children were too young to draw much attention.

It was mid-morning when they finally reached the fortified wooden doors that protected the old stone convent. An elderly nun invited them into the sanctuary, where she placed the babies on the Alter in order to invoke the blessing of Mother Mary as their protector. Jean-Luc commented on the irony of placing Jewish children in a convent for safe-keeping, to which the woman answered that he need only to remember the Jewish background of Jesus Christ and Mother Mary. What better place, she admonished gently, than to put them in the safe bosom of the church?

They left the convent soon after. The woman dropped him off at the train station in the next village. But before he got out of the car, she placed her hand gently on his arm, and took a moment to gaze deeply into his eyes. "Why do you do this dangerous work?" she asked softly. "People are suffering", he answered. She nodded, mute, her beautiful eyes wet with tears. They were united then, for a brief instant, in the profound power of a shared heart-space, and a mission well accomplished.

And then she left Jean-Luc to make his long way back home. It turned out to be the first of many similar missions and he always hoped she would be his accomplice, but he never saw her again. Years later he met a friend who had known her in the Resistance and heard that the children he helped rescue that intense night were the woman's niece and nephew. They were safely shielded by the church and had survived the war.

Jean-Luc marveled then at the young Jewess's courage. He was proud she had put her trust in him for such a precious mission. In the summers when the butterflies traveled over the mountains he was reminded of her, and often wondered what became of her. Sometimes he thought he caught a sense of her on the wind.

Diamond

(bonds relationship, enhances love, associated with the spiritual ideals)

Liora turned away from the Western Wall, her prayers answered. As is so often the case, the answer came from the depths of her experience. She realized she had to go to the meeting, despite how unnerved she was by the old monk's invitation. Courage had rung like a clarion call throughout her soul's journey. She would embrace the opportunity, open to the next twist in her life's adventure.

The next morning, for reasons beyond her, Liora felt a strong need to visit the local mikvah, to purify herself of any residual negative impressions still held in her body. She knew about the ritual of purification of course, and had participated in cleansing rituals in spas around the world, but she had never been to an orthodox Jewish mikvah. The thought of going felt much more to her than mere curiosity ~ instinctively she knew it was essential to the day.

In contrast to the ancient baths Liora had visited at the archeological dig just 20 meters from the Western Wall, the ritual bath currently in use in the Jewish quarter of Old Jerusalem was beautifully tiled in simple beige marble, the still clear water in the bathing pool conducive to the process of purification and renewal.

She decided to participate in the ritual in the traditional way, bathing before entering the ritual pool, making sure to wash well, and comb all her hair free of tangles in order to allow the water to cleanse her without impediment. Then she slowly descended the seven steps into the mikvah pool, lowered herself into the water three times, bending over in order to immerse herself fully. *"Baruch ata adonai eloheinu melech ha-olam she-heche-yanu, ve-ki-y'manu, ve-higi-yanu la-z'man ha-zeh".* Blessed are You, Source of all Life, Who has kept me alive and sustained me, and enabled me to reach this day.......

ꕥ

Kundun was delighted to see the Sheik again. Aside from the joy of their forthcoming conversation about the similarities between their two faiths, he knew the Sheik was an active member of an interfaith peace group with other religious leaders and was intrigued to find out more of this work.

To his delight, the following day, the Sheik told him they would be going to a meeting of that group - the Abrahamic Reunion, he called it. As they drove through the countryside to the meeting, the Sheik talked passionately about the participants. He told Kundun all about the small group of Rabbis, Imams, Sheiks, Priests, Palestinians and Israelis, optimistic men and women who refuse to believe that peace is impossible, and have taken the hard road of working tirelessly to try and bring peace and reconciliation to that embattled part of the world.

Kundun was always disturbed by how polarized the world had become and the blatant self-interest and lack of respect and recognition of differing perspectives he encountered amongst people. All too often he saw people suffering from the pain of disempowerment, and the indignity of colonization. "Yes", he agreed, today one can see the face of polarization on every level ~ global, local, and face to face in the market places and Holy shrines they encountered along the way.

The Peacemakers, the Sheik told him, fully understand how imperative it is to move beyond the constriction and boundaries responsible for the horror and devastation they see perpetrated in the Holy Land. Kundun could feel the Sheik's passion as he emphasized the greatness he saw in the hearts and hopes of the spiritual peacemakers. "They meet God," he said, "through their faith, and through their realization of the illusion of the great divide. But most importantly", he stressed, "they are people who sit in the grit and grind of the aftermath of terror and invite dialogue and real healing."

Kundun and the Sheik agreed with one another that to the extent that human beings ignore the importance of their own particular stories, they are in pain. And to the extent that they ignore the importance of the stories of other people, they perpetuate pain. And that to dominate other people's dreams and way of life, and ignore the gift that can happen when people come together from an honoring place, is to create more pain.

"The Peacemakers," the Sheik stated emphatically, "have seen enough pain. They come together with leaders of different faiths, with political leaders across ideologies, in grassroots handholding, meetings of neighbors, of mothers, of children, of hope, to remind people that we are all intimate and ongoing participants in the creation of the universe and that we have a choice of how to create our reality."

Kundun was glad to hear that the Peacemakers are not simply idealists, but realists who live daily with the tensions of fear and despair, continuing to walk the path of hope and healing despite setbacks and difficulties. When violence erupts between Palestinians and Israelis, they take to the streets holding hands, portraying a powerful message of unity through diversity. They conduct Sulha ~ reconciliation meetings, in parks where members of opposing communities pass olive branches and listen to each other's stories, coming together through their shared pain and confusion. He heard that they create schools for Palestinian and Israeli children, who learn about each other's religions and get to know each other by becoming friends. They arrange tea and knitting parties for women and musical evenings and soccer games for adolescents, bridging together both sides of that bitter fence.

"The truth is", the Sheik emphasized, "the group is aware that their work is to create nothing short of a miracle." For in the tiny moments looking deeply into the eyes, tears and smiles of the so-called other, sharing heartfelt fears, stories, and dreams, they open the way for miracles.

Kundun was open to participating in miracles. He was also aware that the Sheik probably wanted him to report the activities of the group to the Dalai Lama. This was why he was invited.........or so he thought.......

Israel: the meeting

Liora was glad not to be the first to arrive at the meeting. The Rabbi's wife greeted her warmly and if she was surprised to see Liora, she did not show it. The living room was already full of people. It was inviting in its simplicity, obviously a family home, obviously well used to entertaining friends. Immediately the informality and lack of pretense put her at ease.

In one corner sat two women. Liora was gladdened to see an Orthodox Jewish woman, her dress conservative, her head covered by a traditional scarf, chatting easily with a Palestinian woman, just as traditional in her dress and just as modest in her carriage. In another corner stood a group of men, the Rabbi, obvious in his skull cap and long black robe exuding the perfume of a mystic, an Episcopalian Priest, a Druze Sheik with his distinctive white kerchief headdress, and his back to her, the familiar maroon robe of a Tibetan Buddhist monk.

Liora liked the Tibetan monks she had met. She had been blessed to meet His Holiness, The Dalai Lama, when she found herself in Dharamsala at the same time as the 40th year anniversary celebrations for the Tibetan Government in Exile. She happened to be staying with friends in the house of the Raja of Kangra whose jurisdiction housed the Tibetan Government set up in 1959 when His Holiness went into exile. Thanks to the generosity of her illustrious host, she'd found herself sitting front row center in the VIP section at the celebration ceremony.

· The ceremony, which drew enormous press coverage and a huge crowd of well-wishers, took place on the local dusty police grounds. A stage was set up for important government officials of both the Tibetan and Indian Governments. Off to the right of the stage was the covered VIP section in front of which was a large open patch of grass, and beyond that the largest decorated tent Liora had ever seen. In typical Indian fashion it was ornate, festive and held a good few thousand people.

The celebrations went on for many hours. It was hot, the speeches were interminable, and after a while, the VIP seats turned out to be extremely hard. A long back-and-forth discussion of good manners and protocol ensued before she and a friend could take it no longer, and they moved rather unceremoniously to sit more comfortably on the patch of open grass in front of the stage where they could stretch their legs.

The beauty of that "simple monk," as the Dalai Lama calls himself, is that he is, above all else, present and lovingly compassionate to whoever is directly in front of him. Which happened, as Liora and her friend sat on the grass, to have been them. Despite the formalities of the occasion, the Dalai Lama seemed to delight in their decision, although he displayed a certain concern. Every so often he would signal to them to drink more water and cover their heads because of the intensity of the sun.

And at the end of the ceremony, on his way out, he stopped to touch his forehead to hers, take her hands in his, and inquire sincerely about her well-being. His capacity for loving and caring was truly inspiring. She agreed with her friend that, "After a few minutes His Holiness slides away and you meet yourself in your own heart."

ﻍ

And so it was with a feeling of warmth that Liora prepared to greet the Tibetan monk as he turned around......

In retrospect, neither could remember much of the Peace meeting. Of course they remembered in minute detail the moment their eyes met, but the rest of the afternoon was a hazy blur. They remembered that the room fell silent. And in that silence, Liora remembers catching her breath as she looked into his eyes, and the odd feeling she had that she was looking into all of time, and beyond. Kundun too was taken aback. Strangely, he remembered that he had seen her once before some years back in Dharamsala when he was helping with the celebrations for the Tibetan Government's 40th Anniversary. He remembered her, not so much for the insouciance she had to sit on the grass before the stage, although that amused him, but because at that time, he was struck by the beauty of her inner light.

And now here she was again and he could do nothing but reach instinctively for her hand and place it on his heart. In that hushed moment as they looked into each other's eyes, they both recognized something beyond time and space. Somewhere on the periphery of their awareness they heard the invocation: Towards the One, the perfection of Love, Harmony and Beauty..." Their journey ahead shimmered in potential and purpose.

The others in the room witnessing their meeting felt the hushed presence of deep mystery. The shadows of the Druze Sheik melded with the old Greek Orthodox monk and floated across the white wall like a chiaroscuro mirage. The Rabbi felt a palpable quiver like the flitting of a butterfly in his heart. And the two women were aware of a white dove outside the window lift off into the golden late-afternoon sky.

☙

And Indra chuckled as another tear in the firmament began to mend.

Timeline and Character Appendix

Time	*Place*	*Names and roles*	*Names and roles*
Present	**Israel; India, plane**	**Liora**	**Kundun**
Before recorded time	Africa	Hunter - husband	!Knomsie - wife
Before recorded time	France	Mother	Boy
18th Dynasty BCE	Egypt	Ineni - architect	Iset - Priestess
34AD	Judea	Joanna - one of the women	Amina- Beduion
13th C	France	Pere Jean-Baptiste - priest	Anique - healer
1568 AD	India	Sachdeva Khushwant Sharma - student	Mohammad Latif Chisti - teacher
1694 AD	New Mexico	Friar Angelo - priest	Niyol - medicine man
1860 AD	Morocco	Sarah - Jewish woman	Aliyah - Sufi woman
1905 AD	England	Gwyneth - girl	Swami - teacher
1941 AD	Swiss/French/ German Borderlands	Woman - resistance member	Jean-Luc - resistance member

Glossary

Akashic Records: A compendium of mystical knowledge supposedly encoded in a non-physical plane of existence known as the astral plan

Alhamdulillah: Praise be to God.

Allah: Arabic name of God.

Angelic plane: plane of existence inhabited by the angels.

Arduina: Patron goddess of the Ardennes Forest and region, represented as a huntress riding a boar.

Argan oil: A plant oil produced from the kernels of the argan tree endemic to Morocco. The argan tree grows wild in semi-arid soil. The oil is used for food use and cosmetics.

Astral plane: plane of existence postulated by classical (particularly neo-Platonic), medieval, oriental and esoteric philosophies. It is the world crossed by the soul in its astral body on the way to being born and after death.

*Avatamsaka Sutr*a: Recounts the metaphor of Indra's net and was developed by the Mahayana school in the 3rd century. The image of "Indra's net" is used to describe the interconnectedness of the universe.

Avinu Malchienu: Hebrew for "Our Father, our King".

Bardo: Tibetan Buddhist word meaning intermediate or transitional state of existence often between two lives.

Berber: Indigenous people of North Africa west of the Nile Valley.

Bodhisattva: In Buddhism a Bodhisattva is an enlightened being motivated by great compassion.

Brahmin: An individual belonging to the Hindu priest, artists, teachers, and technicians class.

Chenrezig: Tibetan Buddhist name for the Bodhisattva of Compassion.

Chisti lineage: Sufi order within the mystic Sufi tradition. It began in Chisht, a small town near Herat, Afghanistan about 930 CE. The Chishti Order is known for its emphasis on love, tolerance, and openness. Chishti teachers have established centers in the United Kingdom, the United States, Australia and South Africa.

Chrysocolla: blue/green copper cyclosilicate mineral often made into gemstones.

Dalai Lama: is a high lama in the Gelug or "Yellow Hat" school of Tibetan Buddhism, founded by Tsongkhapa (1357–1419). The name is a combination of the Mongolic word dalai meaning "ocean" and the Tibetan word meaning "guru, teacher, mentor". The Dalai Lama is traditionally thought to be a manifestation of the bodhisattva of compassion.

Dharma: Behaviors that include duties, rights, laws, conduct, virtues and "right way of living". In Buddhism it also means "cosmic law and order".

Dhargah: Sufi shrine built over the grave of a revered religious figure, often a Sufi saint or dervish.

Dhikr: is a Sufi term meaning "to remember", it is a devotional act in which short phrases or prayers are repeatedly recited silently or aloud.

Dome of the Rock: A shrine located on the Temple Mount in the Old City of Jerusalem. It was completed in 691 CE. The site's significance stems from religious traditions regarding the rock, known as the Foundation Stone, at its heart, which bears great significance for Jews, Christians and Muslims.

Druze: a monotheistic religious community, found primarily in Syria, Lebanon, Israel and Jordan. Druze beliefs incorporate elements from Abrahamic religions, Gnosticism, Neoplatonism, Pythagoreanism. They highlight the role of the Mind and truthfulness. The Druze call themselves *Ahl al-Tawhid* "the People of Monotheism" or "the People of Unity" or *al-Muwaḥḥidūn* "the Unitarians".

Golgotha, or Calvary: The hill where Christ's crucifixion took place.

Gregorian chants: A form of monophonic, unaccompanied sacred song of the Roman Catholic Church.

Herod Antipas: 1st-century ruler of Galilee, best known his role in events that led to the executions of John the Baptist and Jesus of Nazareth.

Imam: An Islamic leadership position. It is most commonly used in the context of a worship leader of a mosque and Muslim community by Sunni Muslims.

Indra: In the Vedas, Indra is the leader of the Devas or demi gods and the lord of heaven in the Hindu religion.

Iset: Ancient Egyptian patroness of nature and magic.

Jali: A perforated stone screen, with an ornamental pattern using calligraphy and geometry. This form of architectural decoration is found in Indian architecture, Indo-Islamic Architecture and Islamic Architecture.

Kabbalists: Students of the Kabbalah, a set of esoteric teachings meant to explain the relationship between an unchanging, eternal, and mysterious God and the mortal and finite universe (God's creation).

Karma: Refers to the principle of causality where intent and actions of an individual influence the future of that individual.

Khoisan Bushmen: Hunter/gathers, they are the indigenous inhabitants of Southern Africa.

Lapis lazuli: Blue semi-precious gemstone composed of the mineral feldspathoid silicate.

Machpelah: Burial place of Abraham, Isaac, Jacob, Sarah, Rebecca, and Leah, considered the Patriarchs and Matriarchs of the Jewish people.

Magi: Followers of Zoroastrianism or Zoroaster.

Malachite: A green colored copper carbonate hydroxide mineral often used to create jewelry.

Mala beads: A set of beads commonly used by Hindus and Buddhists, usually made from 108 beads used for keeping count while reciting, chanting, or mentally repeating a mantra or the name or names of a deity.

Mandala: A spiritual symbol representing the universe.

Mantra: Sacred utterance, sound, or syllable or group of words believed to have spiritual power.

Maya: Term found in Pali and Sanskrit literature meaning an "illusion" or a "delusion".

Medicine Wheel: Structures constructed by the indigenous peoples of America for religious, ritual, healing, and teaching purposes.

Medina: Distinct city section found in many North African cities, it is typically walled and contains many narrow and maze-like streets.

Meenakari: Persian art of coloring and ornamenting the surface of metals by fusing over it brilliant colors that are decorated in an intricate design. Moghuls spread it to India.

Mikvah: A bath used for the purpose of ritual immersion in Judaism. The word "mikveh", as used in the Hebrew Bible, literally means a "collection" – generally, a collection of water. Several biblical regulations specify that full immersion in water is required to regain ritual purity after ritually impure incidents have occurred.

Moghul: A Persianate empire extending over large parts of the Indian subcontinent and ruled by a dynasty of Chagatai-Turkic origin in the early 16th century.

Muezzin: is the person appointed at a mosque to lead, and recite, the call to prayer (adhan) for every event of prayer and worship.

Murshid: Arabic for "guide" or "teacher". Particularly in Sufism it refers to a Sufi teacher.

Nafs: Arabic word meaning self, psyche or ego. The ego (*nafs*) is considered the lowest dimension of man's inward existence, his animal nature.

Navaho: Largest Native American Nation occupying portions of northeastern Arizona, southeastern Utah, and northwestern New Mexico.

Paganism: Group of indigenous and historical polytheistic religious traditions including any non-Abrahamic, folk, or ethnic religion. Latin Christians adopted it as an all-embracing, pejorative term for polytheists.

Passover: The Passover Seder is a Jewish ritual feast that marks the beginning of the Jewish holiday of Passover. It is a ritual performed by a community or by multiple generations of a family, involving a retelling of the story of the liberation of the Israelites from slavery in ancient Egypt. This story is in the Book of Exodus in the Hebrew Bible.

Peridot: A gem quality magnesium rich olivine green in color.

Pharaoh Thuthmose: Thutmose III was the sixth Pharaoh of the Eighteenth Dynasty, a builder of many temples, and presumed to be the Pharaoh at the time of Moses.

Prehnite: An inosilicate of calcium and aluminium, the translucent gemstones range from light green to yellow, but also colorless, blue or white.

Pueblo: Communities of Native Americans in the Southwestern United States of America.

Qabla: Arabic for midwife.

Qur'an: Literally means "the recitation", is the central religious text of Islam, which Muslims believe to be a revelation from God. Sometimes spelled Koran.

Rabbi: A rabbi is a Jewish teacher of Torah, the First Five books of the Old Testament.

Rosary: The Rosary (from Latin 'rosarium', meaning "Crown of Roses"), is a form of prayer used especially in the Catholic Church or a string of prayer beads used to count the component prayers.

Rosh Hashana: the Jewish New Year.

Sahel: The transition between the Sahara desert to the north and the Sudanian Savanna to the south, it stretches across the southernmost extent of Northern Africa between the Atlantic Ocean and the Red Sea.

Salaam: Arabic word for peace and wholeness.

Samhain: Festival marking the end of the harvest season and the beginning of winter or the "darker half" of the year.

Sarangi: A bowed, short-necked string instrument from South Asia used in Hindustani classical music.

Sephardic: Distinct community of Iberian Jews originating in the Israelite tribes who lived in the Iberian Peninsula from around the turn of the first millennium.

Sekhemet: Goddess of healing for Upper Egypt.

Shalom: Hebrew word for peace and wholeness.

Shekinah: Kabbalistic term for the indwelling of the Divine Spirit on earth.

Sheik: Honorific often used in Islamic countries to describe a spiritual leader, or the patriarch of a tribe or family.

Stations of the Cross: Refers to a series of artistic representations, often sculptural, depicting Christ Carrying the Cross to his crucifixion. The Stations of the Cross originated in pilgrimages to Jerusalem.

Sufi: Practitioner of a perennial philosophy of existence that predates religion, the expression of which flowered within Islam. Sufis strive to experience the Divine Presence at all moments.

Sulha: Arabic for reconciliation.

Swami: An ascetic or yogi or guru who has been initiated into the religious monastic order founded by some religious teacher.

Tadelakt: Moroccan tradition, using lime from The Marrakech Plateau. The word means "to rub in" and olive soap is rubbed into the plaster giving it a beautiful sheen. It is used on both the interior and exteriors of buildings.

Taschlikh: Jewish practice usually performed on the afternoon of the Jewish New Year. The previous year's sins are symbolically "cast off" by reciting a section from Micah that makes allusions to the symbolic casting off of sins, into a large, natural body of flowing water.

Tehuti: Ancient Egyptian god associated with magic and maintaining the universe.

Temple Mount: Site in Jerusalem of the 1st and 2nd Temples, is one of the most important religious sites in the Old City of Jerusalem. It has been used as a religious site for thousands of years and is holy to Jews, Christians and Muslims.

Thanka: a painting on cotton, or silk appliqué, usually depicting a Buddhist deity, scene, or mandala.

Tikkun Olam: A Hebrew phrase that means "repairing the world" (or "healing the world") which suggests humanity's shared responsibility to heal, repair and transform the world.

Tonglen: Buddhist meditation in which one visualizes taking onto oneself the suffering of others on the in-breath, and on the out-breath giving happiness and success to all sentient beings

Tourmaline: A crystal boron silicate mineral classified as a semi-precious stone. The gemstone comes in a wide variety of colors.

Vedas: Large body of texts originating in ancient India. The texts constitute the oldest layer of Sanskrit literature and the oldest scriptures of Hinduism. They are supposed to have been divinely revealed.

Via Dolorosa: A street within the Old City of Jerusalem, held to be the path that Jesus walked, carrying his cross, on the way to his crucifixion.

Wadi: Arabic term traditionally referring to a dry riverbed that contains water during times of heavy rain, or simply an intermittent stream.

Western Wall: The Western Wall, Wailing Wall or Kotel is located in the Old City of Jerusalem at the foot of the western side of the Temple Mount. It is a remnant of the ancient wall that surrounded the Jewish Temple's courtyard, and is arguably the most sacred site recognized by the Jewish faith outside of the Temple Mount itself.

Whirling dervishes: Followers of Jalal ad-Din Muhammad Balkhi-Rumi, a 13th-century Persian poet, Islamic jurist, and theologian. They are also known as the Whirling Dervishes due to their famous practice of whirling as a form of dhikr (remembrance of God). Dervish is a common term for an initiate of the Sufi path.

Yizkor: Memorial prayer for the departed, imploring God to remember the souls of relatives and friends that have passed on, and strengthening the connection between ourselves and the departed souls, bringing them and elevating them in their celestial homes.

Yurt: Portable, round dwelling structure traditionally used by nomads in the steppes of Central Asia.

Zellij: It is one of the main characteristics of Moroccan architecture and consists of geometrical mosaics made of ceramic used mainly as ornament for walls, ceilings, fountains, floors, pools, and tables.

Zhen: Part of a Tibetan Buddhist's robe that is wrapped around his upper body

Zoroaster: also known as Zarathustra was the founder of Zoroastrianism and lived in the eastern part of the Iranian Plateau. Dates proposed in scholarly literature diverge widely, between the 18th and the 6th centuries BCE.

All glossary references are sourced from Wikipedia.

About the Author

Lorell Frysh, PhD, holds a Doctorate in East-West psychology with a focus on spiritual counseling. Her deep immersion in many of the world's spiritual and mystical traditions, and the years she has spent lecturing on this topic renders her highly and uniquely qualified to write *Jewels in the Net of the Gods*.

As a Transpersonal Psychology, Dr. Frysh practices and teaches classes and workshops on spirituality and psychology. She has over 20 years of experience as a past life regression therapist, is a Reverent in the Sufi Order and is on the teaching staff of the Kabbalah Experience and lectures regularly in the Boulder/Denver area.

An eager participant in the richness of life, Dr. Frysh enjoys the benefit of her formal education and thirty five years spent exploring, studying, and receiving initiation in the great spiritual, mystical, and healing traditions of the world. These include Advaita Vedanta, Buddhism, Sufism, Jewish mysticism, Native American Shamanism, Zulu and Venda Shamanism, and time spent with the KoiSan Bushmen of the Kalahari Desert. Her love for the expressions of the world's cultures continues to inspire her Psychology, and Spiritual practices, as well as her writing and teaching.

Dr. Frysh lives in Boulder, CO. The beauty and grandeur of the Rocky Mountains provide daily inspiration, as do frequent trips to visit her two children, and annual visits to spend time in the bush with her family in South Africa.

Keep in touch with Lorell on her website:
www.lorellfrysh.com

Made in the USA
San Bernardino, CA
05 March 2016